BAD MOON RISING

A LOUP GAROU WORLD NOVEL
(TEMPTING FATE)

MANDY M. ROTH

RAVEN HAPPY HOUR, LLC

Published by Raven Books and Raven Happy Hour, LLC
www.ravenhappyhour.com

BLURB

Bad Moon Rising
Tempting Fate: Loup Garou Series Book Two

A Loup Garou World Novel

Gina, a natural-born slayer with a little some-thing special, has been looking for love in all the wrong places. She's not holding out for Prince Charming and for some strange reason, she can't stop having feelings she shouldn't for a man she considers just a friend. Sure, he's hot, but he's an alpha male shifter. Shifters and slayers don't mix. It's just the way of it. Plus, he's been friend zoned.

Detective Jay Gonzales is so in love with the spitfire redheaded slayer he can't see straight. She keeps him at arm's length and he can't blame her. He's got a history as a ladies' man and he's not what her slayer buddies would consider a catch. He doesn't care. She means something to him, and this alpha wolf shifter isn't about to take no for an answer, especially since he's sure she's his mate. Breaking the news to his pack, and keeping her safe from a rising dark threat in the city, are just two more obstacles he has to overcome to make Gina his forever.

TEMPTING FATE SERIES

Tempting Fate Series
Loup Garou
Bad Moon Rising
And more to come!

More coming soon. Visit www.MandyRoth.com
for details.

DEDICATION

To every one of you who have waited since 2007 to read the next book in the series world. Thank you for under- standing the highs and lows of the publishing world and for standing behind me while I worked to get Jay and Gina's story into your hands.

1

I KEPT A FAKE SEXY SMILE PRESSED TO MY FACE as I did my job—policing the supernatural. My current assignment was to gather intel on a new nightclub that had opened in the city. Rumor on the street was the place was run by vampires. I'd already confirmed as much. Not that there was any problem with vamps owning a business, even clubs, but there had been an uptick in violent, supernatural-related deaths in the area. As a slayer, I was there to make sure the place was on the level and wasn't offering an all-you-can-eat buffet of humans, or run by Satan himself.

One never knew.

I'd yet to meet him.

I knew his son—the Prince of Darkness.

He was cool.

Wasn't sure if Daddy was hip as well.

Supernaturals lived among humans without humans ever realizing as much. My boss, Zachariah, was the head of the slayers for the city and had explained more than once what had happened each time throughout history when supernaturals had been discovered. After countless lectures on the matter, I knew that bad, bad things had happened. He liked to blame the Dark Ages on it all. I liked to nod and try to get out of hearing any more about the topic.

The club's music was extra loud, and it made me wonder if the fact I thought as much meant I was getting old. Glancing around, I realized I wasn't any older than most of the patrons. My deep-cut, fit-and-flare red dress fit right in with what other women were wearing to the upscale club. I'd paired the dress with four-inch heels, adding height to my five-foot-six-inch frame. While the heels fit the party scene, they weren't exactly practical in my line of work.

Nothing I was wearing was mine.

Zachariah kept a vast roomful of clothing

that might be needed by the slayers. The dress had been pulled from there.

I sat on a stool at the bar while observing my surroundings, keeping an eye on the vampires I could see, looking for signs that things weren't quite right. So far, other than a lot of trips to the back feeding room with women who looked as if they charged by the hour, nothing had stuck out. I was ready to go home. So far, I'd been hit on by six different vampires, and three really smarmy humans who actually made the vampires look like great picks.

There had been a time, not that long ago, when I'd have been happy to spend an entire night at a club such as this one, getting hit on by hot men. Things had changed for me recently, but I wasn't sure why.

All I knew was each time a hot guy, living or dead, approached me, trying to buy me drinks and sweet-talk me out of my panties, the idea of letting them touch me nearly sent me into a panic. I'd never had a problem with random hookups before. In fact, I preferred them.

But not now.

As if on cue, a tall man with long dark hair approached, his blue-gray gaze centered on me.

Everything about him said rich and powerful. His deep blue suit was tailored to fit him perfectly, and no doubt cost a pretty penny. I had to admit, the man wore it well. The baby-blue shirt he'd paired with the suit was unbuttoned a bit, showing off his alabaster chest. He had a great body. The new me admired his hotness, but I didn't want to grab a cab and head to a hotel with him like the old me would have wanted to do.

Okay, what the old me would have *already* done.

Everything about the man screamed vampire. The way he seemed to almost glide through the crowd, parting them with ease, his gaze never leaving me, was a big sign he was more than human. The fact he was flawless to look at was another sign. Most vampires that I'd met over the years were suave to the point they didn't even need to bother with sweet-talking a woman out of anything. Women simply threw articles of clothing at them.

I bit my lower lip, hoping he wasn't coming to talk to me.

The closer the vampire got, the more I could sense how dominant he was. He wasn't like the others who had approached me over the past hour. They'd all had a dangerous vibe to them, which all vampires had, but this one screamed master and something else. Something that I couldn't put my finger on.

I was extremely happy I'd decided to use the perfume mixture my boss had made me. Since my boss was a super-friggin'-old vampire himself, he knew certain scents confused his senses, making him unable to detect another supernatural with any sort of ease.

It would do me no good to show up to survey the place if I smelled of slayer to the vampires there. Some didn't have an issue with what I did for a living. But some living-challenged folks clung to the old ways.

When it was us against them.

Good versus evil and that other crap.

Vamps versus slayers.

The master vampire eased in close to me, going to the stool next to mine that had been occupied only seconds before his arrival. I didn't doubt he'd used his power to strongly encourage the person who had been in the seat to get up and move. Luckily the person had, because the master vampire didn't seem like the type who took no for an answer.

He didn't sit, so much as he leaned on the edge of the stool, giving him that too-cool-for-school factor. He faced me, putting one of his long legs out, blocking me from exiting from that side. Had I not been on the current kick of apparently all but giving up my sex drive, I'd have thought the guy was hot.

Very hot.

He motioned to the bartender and then tapped the bar top. "Give the lady another drink."

I licked my lips. A fake smile appeared on my face. It was one I'd perfected over the years. "Thank you, but I'm good."

"I insist," he said, notes of a French accent to his voice. Shamelessly, he pushed my long, dark red hair over my shoulder, his fingers gliding over my skin in the process. "Tell me why it is someone as beautiful as you has been sitting here *alone* for over an hour. And why you have turned down a number of other men."

I kept calm even though I wanted to shiver at his touch. "I'm meeting someone."

He skimmed a long finger over my bare

upper arm, all the while his gaze fixed on the deep cut of my dress. I knew it showed part of my breasts since it was open to just above my navel. That had seemed like a great idea before I went to the club. You know, keep the guys, dead or not, focused on my boobs and not my face, just in case I bumped into one while on patrol.

Being recognized by a vampire was an occupational hazard. Now the dress seemed like the worst idea I'd had lately, and I'd drank orange juice after I brushed my teeth when I woke for the day.

The vampire leaned in towards me, and it was all I could do to stay on the stool and not thrust him away. He wasn't what he appeared to be. He was something more, something darker.

"Is your gentleman caller late?" he asked, his voice sliding over me like butter even though he leaked darkness.

"Yes," I said, keeping my tone light and sexy. "He'll be here soon. I'm sure he got held up with work. This isn't really like him."

"I can think of a variety of things to do if he does not appear," the vampire said, standing and easing me off the bar stool, his hands finding my waist.

He was over six feet tall, leaving him standing a good deal taller than me. Most supernatural males were freakishly tall. I swear there was something in the water that made them all grow over six feet—and be sexy as hell.

He drew me in towards him as he licked his lips. "You are simply divine."

I stared up at him.

He eased me in the direction of the dance floor, and I hesitated. It was clear he was the guy in charge because it was very rare to have more than one master vampire hanging out together, two powerful beings rarely liked sharing the spotlight. I could learn more from him about what was going on in the area than anyone else. I could also end up having to fight a master vampire, which was harder than dusting the normal ones. And everything about the man near me said he'd be very hard to take down.

There was something else that bothered me about him. More than the added darkness even, and I couldn't put my finger on it. But I did start to feel out of my depth near him.

I hedged as he continued to walk in the

direction of the dance floor. "I don't think I should. My boyfriend might not really approve."

The vampire touched my chin, forcing me to meet his gaze, something a normal human should avoid at all cost. "Any man who would permit you to come to a club alone and then leave you waiting any length of time is not a man worth your worry or your concern. I can promise you a most enjoyable night. Come, let me show you pleasure like you've never known."

I had to hand it to him, he was so *humble*.

Cutting my losses and leaving the club sounded great, but if the vampires at the club had something to do with the rise in violent crimes in the area, I needed to know. My job was to protect the innocent, and sometimes that meant I had to do things I didn't want to.

Like dance with the super-sexy vampire with undertones of evil.

He licked his lips. "I see no boyfriend here. What he doesn't know will not hurt him."

Giving in, I nodded and let him lead me deeper onto the dance floor. The song changed to one that had a substantial beat accompanied by the sounds of sex. It pumped through the club.

I was sure the master vampire had a hand in the song change and choice. My brow quirked, and he chuckled softly.

Yep. He was guilty.

He then drew me against him and began to move in a way that surprised me. For some reason, I didn't expect him to be much of a dancer. I was wrong. Very wrong. I moved with him, trying to glance around to watch for suspicious activity. He was so tall and big that it was hard to see much beyond him.

One of his hands went to my hip and the other he tried to run down my chest.

Catching his hand, I shook my head no.

He grinned, his look screaming "challenge accepted."

He dipped his head going to my neck area. It took all of me to avoid tensing. His lips found my ear and spoke. "What is your name?"

"Gina," I said, surprised I'd blurted out my real name—or the shortened version of my real name.

He kept his lips near my ear. "I am Reynaud."

My hands went to his chest in an attempt to put space between us. It didn't work.

The next I knew, he was moving my hair back from my neck, putting his face close to it.

This time I did tense. "This feels wrong," I said, hoping to find an out. "I'm sure this would upset my boyfriend. As nice as this is, he means a lot to me. I don't want to hurt him."

There was no boyfriend.

"Gina, I can give you so much pleasure. Beyond anything he could hope to hold a candle to."

Yep. Totally humble.

I eased back a touch more. "Thank you for the offer, Reynaud, but I'm not willing to throw away what I have with him for a night of bliss with you."

His gaze held a hunger that was actually disconcerting. "It does not have to be one night of bliss. It can be hundreds of years' worth."

2

OUT OF NOWHERE, THE CLUB'S TEMPERATURE seemed to increase as heat pulsed over me, warning me of danger and exciting me. I knew the power wasn't from Reynaud. I sensed something powerful, alpha, and pissed close by. It wasn't a vampire, but it was a force to be reckoned with. I was sure of that.

Turning, I spotted Jayson "Jay" Gonzales about three feet behind me. I'd known him for years and trusted him fully. He had a presence that demanded attention. It didn't hurt that he had an endless supply of muscles, making him hard all over. It wasn't as if he looked overdone like some of those bodybuilder guys in the banana huggers who put on too much self-tanner and then flexed their freakish bulging muscles accompanied by popping veins.

No. Jay was built with a perfect ratio.

His black hair that was longer on top and shorter on the sides had gel in it tonight, looking messy yet stylishly so. His chiseled jawline had a light dusting of dark facial hair, which only made him sexier. The black long-sleeved shirt he wore was cuffed on his forearms with the top unbuttoned enough to show off his steely chest. He had on a pair of dark jeans and black biker boots.

He looked great.

Too great.

At that moment, he looked like a lifeline, and I wasn't about to pass up on the chance to put distance between myself and Reynaud. I may be able to beat the crap out of almost any supernatural, but I'm not stupid. Reynaud was tripping all my inner slayer alarms. I'd be a fool to ignore the warnings.

Jay's deep brown gaze locked on the vampire behind me. From Jay's expression, he wasn't happy. In fact, he looked like he might attack someone, which would be very bad in a club full of vampires.

Unsure what Jay's problem was, and needing to avoid a big scene, I smiled wide at him, hoping to head off any problems. "You made it!"

His gaze slid to me and heated instantly.

This time I blushed, and it was for real.

I went to him fast and leaped at him.

He caught me and held me off my feet, leaving me able to put my lips to his ear. "Play nice."

He tightened his hold as I trailed kisses over his cheek to his full lips in an attempt to make it look like he really was the man I'd been waiting for. I was about to wiggle to get down when Jay surprised me, taking hold of my mouth with his. He thrust his tongue into my mouth, and my nipples hardened instantly.

I moaned and returned the kiss tenfold. My entire body lit with need, and I had to force myself to stop kissing him. For a second, I was too shaken by what happened to comment. Two deep breaths later, I had my hormones under control enough to form a sentence. "Mmm, I was starting to think you forgot about me."

He didn't even bother to help with the act. Instead, Jay kissed me again.

I had to push on his chest a good deal to get him to stop when in truth, I wanted him to continue. When finished, I let out a nervous giggle, sounding like some of the bubble-headed chicks who had been at the bar near me earlier.

Jay set me down gently and took my hand in his as he cast the vampire a look that screamed "mine." Guiding me through the club, he walked me right into one of the many small rooms in the back. I'd been to enough vampire clubs to know the rooms were used for sex and feeding, which generally went hand in hand.

I glanced around to find a chaise lounge there. Decorative pillows were on the floor against the wall to the right. The walls were painted blood red, which was ironic when one thought about it. And sound-absorbing panels were placed strategically, no doubt to block screams.

"Is anyone listening?" I asked, knowing his shifter hearing was far superior to a slayer's.

"No," he said, his breathing hard.

"Where's your date?" I asked, knowing Jay liked the ladies. "I'm sorry I pulled you away from her. I'll explain the kissing bit. Sorry."

He touched my cheek. "I'm here alone."

I lifted a brow. "For real?"

He nodded.

"Jay, you're smart enough to know this club doesn't cater to your kind. I've only seen a handful of shifters here tonight and the vibe they've let off is not great."

As an alpha wolf shifter, he knew as well as I did that vamps and shifters often refused to play nicely together.

"I know what this place is. Imagine my surprise when I got a call telling me you were here by yourself."

"What? Why would someone call you to report where I'm at?" I asked.

He ignored my question, only to pose one of his own. "You on the prowl for a bloodsucker to spend the night with? That what you're into now? I thought better of you, Gina."

I'd have taken offense if I didn't sense his concern for me. "Jayson, I'm working. I'm here checking out the club to report back to Zachariah. I'm not on the prowl for anyone or anything, or did you miss the way I threw myself at you to get away from Reynaud?"

He exhaled slowly, relief showing on his face.

"I'd have called you if I wanted to go out clubbing and this place wouldn't have been my first choice," I stressed, my gut telling me he needed to hear that. "I've been here over an hour doing my best to turn down a seemingly endless line of guys who do nothing for me. Well, the last one gave me a hinky vibe. He's more than what he looks like."

Jay drew me against him. "You shouldn't be here alone. They would gang up on you and tear you apart if they knew what you really are."

I put my hand on his chest. "Jay, one of them will smell what *you* are if we go back out there. You don't let off a dark vibe. They'll tear you apart too."

"I'm not worried about me," he said, keeping me close.

I couldn't look away from him. "I worry about you."

For a second, neither of us said a word.

I glanced around the room. "Well, since we have the place to ourselves, how about we get naked and rub all over each other?"

Jay stiffened. "Gina?"

"Relax. I was joking. Kind of. I want you safe, so you need to take a seat."

He didn't budge.

I yanked on Jay, tapping into my slayer strength so that I could move him. I pushed him back and onto the chaise. He landed on his butt, sitting upright, his feet on the floor, his back to the wall. Wasting no time, I climbed onto his lap, straddling him. I then unbuttoned his shirt, pushing it open.

"Gina!" he said, trying and failing to get me off him. "Are you trying to make me lose control here?"

"I'm trying to mask your scent with mine. Zachariah gave me something to help hide what I am," I said, laughing at him. "Now, rub yourself against me until my scent covers your wolf."

He licked his lips and smirked as he stopped trying to escape. He took hold of my hips, settling in nicely. "It's like Christmas and my birthday all wrapped into one."

I'd have laughed if I wasn't so worried that he'd end up a one-man blood bank to the vamps in the club. "Jayson, hurry."

He reached between us and adjusted himself. "Baby, the problem is going to be getting me to slow down. Not hurry."

Used to his humor, I sat up and eased the

front of my already low-cut dress open more. "Okay, get to getting here, buddy."

He thumped his head against the wall as his hands found my exposed thighs, making my body heat even more. "Gina, I'm pretty sure I had this exact fantasy when I was a teenager. Okay, I had it yesterday, too."

"Having a chick on your lap?" I asked with a laugh. "Somehow I think you've made that a reality quite a few times in your life."

His gaze locked on mine. "Having a hot redhead on me, pressing her chest against my face."

Groaning, I tugged on his shoulders, as the darkness I'd sensed from Reynaud seemed to permeate through the wall. "Jay, please."

Jay drew me to him more, his hands sliding higher on my thighs as his face pressed to my neck first. His lips skimmed my skin, and suddenly I wasn't so sure having him mask his scent by using me was such a great idea.

He'd become my secret obsession over the past several months, but I couldn't figure out why. I'd known him for years and had never been sexually attracted to him before. It was as if someone had flipped a switch on my sex drive and suddenly, it only had eyes for Jay.

The only real issue was Jay cycled through women like there was no tomorrow. Well, he *had* cycled through them. I hadn't noticed him around any women in the last several months or so, but I didn't spend every hour of every day with him either.

Anything was possible.

Jay lifted me slightly.

I took a moment to wrap my arms around his head, effectively leaving his face right between my breasts. Thankfully my groin was off his, or it might have gotten very damp down there, very fast.

"Yep, my lucky day," he said against my chest.

As he covered himself with my scent, or rather the smell of the perfume on me, it was all too easy for me to picture myself naked on him.

When I realized he was more than covered enough to mask the scent of his wolf but was still going, I cleared my throat. "Jay?"

He kept his head where it was. "Yeah?"

"You're going to rub my skin raw with your

facial hair," I said, liking the fact he wasn't in a hurry to leave the spot.

He released me and sighed as I eased off his lap. His gaze was hungry. "Willing to let me rub you raw with my facial hair in other areas?"

I lost it, laughing as I righted my dress. "We'll save that bucket list item for another day."

He stood painfully slowly and then he reached for my hand. "Okay, I forgot why the hell we're here. All I can think about is how hard my dick is. I know I was pissed about something. I'm sure of it."

"I'm here to gather intel. You're here because someone tattled to you about me being here," I said.

"Still just thinking about how hard my dick is."

I chuckled.

"For real, this isn't a safe place. Fuck what Zachariah wants."

"What if more innocents are hurt because of something happening here?" I questioned, knowing he wanted innocents safe as much as me. Maybe more.

"The pack has their eye on this place."

"How many pack members have gained entrance?" I gave him a pointed stare.

Jay glanced away. "So far, me, here and now."

I took a deep breath. "I'm pretty sure if I walk back out there and we pretend to get into a tiff, the master vampire here, Reynaud, will take me behind the scenes. I can see the inner workings and get a better idea of what's happening around here."

Jay's eyes began to fill with flecks of amber, indicating his wolf was surfacing. "No."

"He gives me the creeps, and something deep down says I don't want to have to go head to head with him but, Jay, I couldn't live with myself if he has something to do with the rise in violence around here and I did nothing about it."

He backed me up against the door and put his hands to both sides of my head, his eyes still holding amber flecks. "You are not to go near him again. If you do, I'll shift fucking forms in the middle of the club. Fuck who sees me."

My gaze hardened. "Jayson, you're being unreasonable."

He snorted. "Me? Uh, try another one,

sweetheart. I'm the only one thinking clearly here. I smelled something more on him the second I entered this place. There is no way in hell I'm allowing him near you again. You can get pissy all you want. In the end, I'll carry you out of here over my shoulder kicking and screaming if need be."

I knew Jay well enough to know he wasn't bluffing. He'd do it without thinking twice.

Grunting, I went to push him away, but the second I made contact with his bare chest, I found myself caressing it lightly. So not what I'd intended to do. Damn him for being so sexy.

"Gina?" he asked, his hand moving over mine.

"Shut up, Jay," I snapped. "If you don't like it, button your shirt. How can I be expected to argue with you when your hard, really well-defined chest is right there, close enough to touch?"

The slightest of smiles formed on his face. He undid the rest of his buttons and put his arms out wide. "Touch your fill. Really, take your time. I find myself in less of a hurry to get you out of here right this second. Fuck the vampires."

With a groan, I rolled my eyes. "Button up there, Casanova."

He did, but he buttoned his shirt all wrong while he stared at my chest.

I knew my little lap dance had teased his inner wolf and that was why he was acting so horny. It was to be expected with alphas. It had nothing to do with him actually wanting to be with *me*.

Not that I could judge him for that. Right now, I wanted to push him down and continue the dance only this time without clothes.

Damn your natural pheromones, Jay. How is a girl supposed to think straight?

Taking pity on him, I took over, buttoning his shirt correctly for him, leaving the top few buttons undone as he'd had them before.

He sniffed the air, his eyes moving from dark brown to amber as he tapped into his wolf more. He jerked me against him and nodded to the door as he lifted three fingers before touching his ear.

I was a great Jay interpreter.

There were three vampires on the other side of the door, listening in on us.

"Uh, there, right there," I said in a low

voice. "Oh, gods! Come with me. Right there. Yes!"

Jay licked his lips, trying to avoid laughing at my antics.

"Ah, baby," he said, his voice deep. "Don't fucking move. Fuck! You have got to stop doing that thing with your hips if you want me to last longer."

It was my turn to crack up. I had to slap my hand over my mouth to keep from making noise.

"Guess we should get back out there before people figure out what we're doing in here," he said. "Ready?"

Nodding, I pulled my dress slightly, partially exposing more of my breasts. I tousled my hair, doing my best to look like I'd just banged Jay. My hand found Jay's as I gave a sultry laugh.

He drew me away from the door and opened it, putting his body in front of mine as we headed out of the room.

"That was worth waiting for you tonight," I said, easing around him while ignoring him squeezing my hand to get me to stop.

Jay was right. Three men were there, looking as if they were having a conversation, but I knew better. All their gazes went to my chest.

Maybe my plan on the dress wasn't as horrible as I'd thought.

"Baby, wait a second," said Jay, easing up behind me, his hand sliding around me and finding my partially exposed breasts. He fixed my dress.

My gaze met the vampires', and I bit my lower lip. "Oops."

Darkness circled my feet first, working its way up my legs. I recognized the source.

Reynaud.

I had to hand it to him. He was persistent.

At that moment, every inner alarm I had went off like there was a five-alarm fire. I knew better than to ignore the warning. My gut feelings had saved my life more than once over the years. And they were something that other slayers I'd met to date didn't possess to the level I did.

"Jay?" I asked, wondering if he felt the darkness creeping up to him as well.

He pulled me against him on the dance floor. He spun me around, putting my back to his front. When he began to move, I stiffened.

Every time I'd seen Jay dancing with someone, he'd looked bored and barely moved. That was not the case now.

It was hard to keep my mind on the task at hand with Jay grinding against me. I fell into sync naturally with him, as if we did this all the time.

We didn't.

I had to force myself to keep looking around the club, trying to get a full read on the situation before we hightailed it out of there. Even I wasn't crazy enough to want to take them all on by myself.

I noticed a fair number of vampires coming and going from a door I'd not seen from the bar. There were too many going in and out for it to be another feeding room.

A tall, burly vampire stood guard at the door, dressed in standard-issue bouncer attire. All black.

Glancing up and behind me, I met Jay's gaze, and he nodded as if reading my mind. Something was beyond that door that was important. His arms wrapped around me and he tugged me tighter against his frame.

Jay kissed the side of my head, his mouth finding my ear. "We can go now."

I nodded, but neither one of us stopped dancing. I turned my head, and Jay jerked me hard to him, the lowest of growls coming from him.

The massive press of darkness hit me hard, and when I looked straight ahead, I found myself staring directly at Reynaud. I'd never heard him approach.

Jay held me to him in a death grip, his entire body coiling. He'd attack soon.

Reynaud's gaze moved up me slowly. He looked up and stared at Jay. "Your girlfriend is exquisite. I find myself drawn to her. Hold her close. You never know when another will snatch her away from you."

I planted my body firmly, afraid Jay would try to charge Reynaud. It would be a very Jay thing to do. As a wolf shifter, his temper was always there, just below the surface.

Jay surprised me by staying where he was. He slid his arms around me more, splaying his hands over my stomach. "Oh, I'm well aware of just how special she is. I plan to hold on to her and never let her go. I wouldn't want to be the person who tried to take her from me."

Twisting, I hugged Jay. "Can we get some fresh air?"

"Of course, baby." He stared past me at Reynaud, and while no threats were outwardly made, they were implied, not to mention Jay's look said it all. He wanted to rip Reynaud's head off.

I pushed more on his chest. "Hon."

Nodding, he laced his fingers through mine, holding my hand as he led me through the club to the entrance. Jay kept going around the exterior of the club to the parking area.

He all but dragged me behind him.

My gaze moved in the direction of the far corner of the club's parking area. Three men were there, watching the club, their attention whipping to Jay and myself. The man in the center had ink-black hair that hung freely down and over his shoulders. He stared right at me, his green gaze familiar. He rubbed his medium-length beard but didn't look away.

Neither did I.

At least not until Jay jerked me around in front of his large black SUV. It was one of a number of vehicles and modes of transportation I'd seen him with.

He ran his hands up and into my hair. "Baby, my place or yours?"

I realized then that he sensed someone listening in. "Mine."

He touched my cheek. "I'm sorry I was late. Work held me up. It won't happen again. And to be clear, if that swanky bastard with the girl hair tries to take you from me, I'll fucking kill him."

My eyes widened. "Jayson!"

Jay shrugged, his hands going to my ass. He gave my backside a good squeeze as he yanked me against him hard. "You're fucking killing me. I'm about to put on a show if we don't get out of here."

I trusted him enough to follow his lead. He helped me into his SUV. My Jeep was parked a ways from the club. He shut the door and walked around, getting in himself. He started the vehicle and pulled out, taking his time to avoid suspicion.

Music from the band Loup Garou blasted through the high-end sound system. Jay turned it down, and I grinned.

"Busted. I knew you liked them."

He cast me a sideways look. "They grow on you."

We knew the band well, especially its frontman, Exavier Kedmen—or Xavier if you asked his wife, my best friend Lindsay…also known as Jay's ex.

When Jay was on the road and a bit away from the club, he looked at me. "Why in the fuck would Zachariah send you into an entire den of vampires alone?"

I blinked. "What? No. It's just a club. Not an actual den."

3

JAY WHITE-KNUCKLED THE WHEEL AS HE continued to drive away from the vampire nightclub. "Gina, I could hear and smell a mass of vampires under the club the minute that guarded door opened and closed. There's a den hidden under there. My guess is there were fifty or more of them in the den, not counting the ones in the club."

It was hard to hide my surprise. "Jay, I can't handle anywhere near that many alone. I don't know any slayer who could."

He hit the wheel and growled. "I fucking know! The second I heard you were heading to a spot my pack has been watching for weeks, I couldn't get to you fast enough. All I could think was I'd show up to find they had torn you to shreds when they figured out you're a slayer."

I'd never been a fan of people worrying about me. It made me feel uncomfortable. No doubt it stemmed from my childhood, but I didn't want to delve deeper. All I knew was the idea of Jay being worked up over my safety made my chest tight. I didn't like seeing him this emotional.

In an attempt to calm him, I put my hand on his arm gently. "Thanks for coming. I didn't mean to freak you out. I know you're busy. My Jeep is a few blocks up. Just drop me there, and you can go back to what you were doing."

"You expect me to drop you off and leave you alone? Uh, no. That master dickwad was interested in you enough to send three of his minions to listen at the door to our feeding room. Even you had to notice his unnatural interest in you. He basically came right out and threatened to take you from me. I will rip his already dead head off him if he lays one finger on you." Jay's jaw was tight. "Why in the fuck would the head of the slayers send one girl in? Does he want you returned in small pieces?"

Jay had always watched out for my friends

and me, but this wasn't normal. He hadn't reacted this way to Myra.

Myra and Jay frequently got along fine. They were both shifters, though she was a cat shifter and he was a wolf shifter. And Myra didn't actually get into trouble or binds. She was straightlaced.

He and my close friend Lindsay had dated for a while. She'd spent a chunk of her adult life being hunted by big dark baddies who knew she was the mate to the Prince of Darkness. Jay, Myra, and I had all tried to look out for her and keep her safe. Exavier, the frontman for Loup Garou—who also happened to be the Prince of Darkness—had reconnected with Lindsay again just over six months ago. Lindsay no longer lived in the city and was six months pregnant— yeah, they'd wasted no time getting busy on the baby making.

That left me. While Jay had always seemed protective of me, he'd never been like this. He'd never been this worked up before. I wasn't exactly sure how to handle it. The me of old would have laughed at him and ignored him. The new me understood he had feelings too.

Yeah. I was broken for sure.

"Jay, I'm okay. I'm out of there now. Thank you for that," I said softly, trying to calm him down. "I'm sure Zachariah didn't realize it was a den in addition to a club. He wouldn't have sent me alone. Just drop me off at my Jeep, and I'll be out of your hair tonight."

"Out of my hair?" he shouted, and gripped the wheel to the point I thought he'd rip it off.

With as strong as he was, he could tear apart the SUV with ease.

I licked my lower lip. Jay and I had been spending a great deal of time together over the past six months. Far more time than we'd ever spent together before. And all of it had been just him and me. At first it was strange, no longer having Myra and Lindsay there as buffers. But then it grew on me. I now looked forward to our time together. To seeing him and just getting to hang out with him. I also understood I was using him to fill the void my best friends had left in their wake.

"I've eaten up a lot of your time already by being at your house nearly daily. And you just drove all the way across the city to get me out of a vampire den. So yes, I want to get out of your hair. You're so busy. You didn't need this tonight too."

He shot me a look that said we were far from done with the conversation. "That dress barely covers you."

"Gee, sorry, *Dad*," I mocked.

"Gina," he growled. "Don't joke about this. You walked into a den of vampires dressed like a present for them to unwrap. You had to fucking know the master would notice you. That he'd take an interest in you. Hell, he'd notice you dressed in a paper bag. You're kind of hard not to notice. The dress you're in demands attention. He was undressing you with his mind. I know it."

I lifted a brow. "So, it's my fault that Reynaud took an interest in me because I dared to wear this dress?"

Jay let out a long, frustrated breath. "Fuck, baby. No. I'm just…I knew you were in there, alone with all of them, and I was terrified I wouldn't get to you in time to get you out. I called Zachariah. He and I both tried calling you. You didn't answer your damn phone."

I'd never seen him this way before. "Um, not to draw more attention to the dress, but where, exactly, was I supposed to put my phone?"

The look he gave me made me wonder if he was going to pull over, spank me, and then send me to my room. Instead, he grabbed my hand and squeezed it tight.

"Can you try not to scare the hell out of me again?" he requested, need showing on his handsome face.

The sincerity in his voice kept me from making a witty comeback. His concern was real, and I had to admit that made warmth spread through me.

"Yes. I'm sorry."

"It's not your fault. I'm taking this out on you when I should be directing my anger at Zachariah." He kept hold of my hand. "I told him to run your missions past me first. I'd have never signed off on this one."

I clenched his hand tightly. "You did what?"

Jay adjusted in his seat nervously. "Nothing. Hey, great dress."

"Jayson, what did you do?" I asked, my voice barely there as I attempted to keep a lid on my anger.

Guiltily, he glanced in my direction. "I *might*

have been talking to Zachariah on a totally unrelated incident, and I *may* have asked that he please keep me updated on what he had you doing. I only asked out of curiosity. Nothing more."

His explanation bordered on ridiculous, so much so that I had to dig deep to find righteous indignation and not merely laugh at him.

"Jayson."

"Give me this, Gina. I worry. The network and support system that were in place between you, Myra, and Lindsay isn't there anymore— not like it was. You're all going in three different directions with your lives now, which is fine. And I know you love each other like sisters, but what happens if you need backup or help in any way?"

"I'm not the only slayer, Jay," I stressed. "Zachariah would send other slayers to me."

He lifted a brow as he glanced at me. "You know as well as I do that you and the rest of the city's slayers have a tense, relationship, at best. I'm sorry. That doesn't work for me when it comes to your safety. And how would you call them when you don't take your phone with you?"

He had a point. I didn't like it. But I couldn't deny he was right.

The other slayers and I did our jobs, but we didn't hang out, chitchat, or like each other much. I'd felt like an outsider when I came on. That hadn't changed despite how long I'd been with the branch. They had their cliques, and I wasn't included in them.

"Fine. Thank you for trying to keep track of me to keep me safe," I said, having to bite back the taste of vinegar from admitting as much. "I'll tell you what, how about you and I do what I used to do with the girls?"

He grinned, and it was entirely too sexy. "Tell me this involves pillows, frilly panties, and whipped cream."

I snorted. "Totally. That all happens before we rub each other down with body lotion."

"Yes!" he said, winking at me. "Sorry. I'll be serious. What are you proposing?"

"That you and I text each other, letting one another know what we're doing, where we are, and that we're okay. Basically, we had updates going all day, in order to be sure each of us was okay. But I doubt you're going to want to be checking in with me all day like I'm your ball and chain or something."

Jay lifted my hand, reminding me he was still holding it. "I love the idea. It's a deal."

I tried to work my hand from his, but he held tight. "Uh, let's add the rule that you and I don't go to the extreme the girls and I did though."

"And that would be?" he asked.

I took a deep breath. "Letting each other know if we're going on a date, or we're going to go back to a guy's house with him, how the sex was, if we're too hungover to move, and so on. I don't want to know about your booty calls." The thought of Jay being with another woman bothered me way more than it should, and it had for months.

The lowest of growls came from him. "No. I say we leave that caveat there."

"Jay, I really do *not* want to know about your sex life," I said earnestly. The very idea of him having one turned my stomach.

"We do this all the way," he returned.

I groaned. "Okay, but I might cut your man parts off if you go into detail about what happened in the bedroom on your dates."

His lips twitched. "You'll let me know if you're going out with anyone, or anything else, right?"

"Sure, but you're going to think I'm not holding up my end of the deal," I confessed, my hand still in his.

"Why is that?"

"Jay, I haven't gone on a date in months. Myra and I were talking about it last week before she left for her mother's, and she pointed out that I haven't been on a date or had a random hookup since right after Exavier and Lindsay mated. So, like six months now. Let me be the first to say, a world record for me."

Jay exhaled slowly, some of the tension in him leaving. "Good."

"What?"

He shook his head. "Nothing."

"What about you? Should I expect eight different texts a day about your newest girl of the moment?" I asked, hoping that wouldn't be the case. "And please do not date that one chick who thought your pager going off was the door-bell. I'm very ashamed *for* you over that one."

He snickered. "Yeah, I'm ashamed over *all* of them. And no, you won't be getting multiple texts from me about women. I, uh, haven't been out with anyone since before Xavier and Lindsay hooked up.

"Jayson, are you dying of something terminal?" I asked, only partially kidding. The man was legendary with his conquests.

"Totally serious."

I tensed. "Is it because you're still hurt over things ending with you and Lindsay?"

He caressed my hand with his thumb. "Gina, that ended long before she and Exavier became an item. And it wasn't a relationship. I need *you* to understand that."

I just looked at him, unsure why he felt the need to stress as much to me.

He pulled off into the empty parking lot of an office building and put the SUV in park. "Gina, I need you to hear me fully. Lindsay and I weren't in love. We weren't even dating."

"Just fucking?" I asked, my chest tightening. I pressed the same fake smile to my face that I'd used with the vampires at the club.

"Dammit," he whispered under his breath. "I didn't know then, Gina."

"Didn't know what?"

Tipping his head back, he looked strained.

"I didn't have all the facts. I was confused. When Exavier pulled me aside after Lindsay's baby shower to talk to me…it all made sense. I'd felt it for years, but I'd talked myself out of it. It all aligns now. I get it. Please know if I could take away my past, what I did and who I did it with, I would."

I had no idea what he was talking about. "You are so incredibly weird, Detective Gonzales."

"I'm trying very hard to tell you I'm sorry," he supplied.

"For what?"

He swallowed hard. "It's complicated."

I snorted. "Okay, my weird, weird friend. I can walk to my car. It's just over a couple of blocks from here. Thanks again for coming for me."

He scowled.

I got out of the SUV and leaned back in for a second. "Hey, are we still meeting at your place tomorrow to work on your kitchen?"

"Gina, I told you, I'm not leaving you alone after the interest I saw that master vampire take in you." Jay leveled a hard gaze on me.

His phone rang, and I knew the ringtone

meant it was work. He sighed and answered the phone. "Gonzales."

I stood there, watching as he rubbed his head.

"Send Taylor," he said with another big sigh. "Romeo, I'm all the way across town. Send fucking Taylor. I know it's my case. Yes, I know Taylor is an asshole. Let him have it. Fine. I'm coming."

He put his phone down and looked at me. "Get in. You're coming with me."

"Jay, I'm fine. You're needed at work."

He reached for me. "Gina."

I winked. "I'm getting my Jeep and heading to Zachariah's. I'll take one of the extra rooms and bunk there for the night. Feel better?"

He exhaled. "I'd feel better if you were bunking at my house, but yes, that's better than you going straight home. Where is your Jeep?"

I pointed to a lot close to us. That wasn't it, but he'd never leave if he knew I'd have to walk a whole three blocks all by myself.

"Gina, remember our deal. Text me the second you get to Zachariah's."

"Will do," I said as I shut the door and walked in the direction of my Jeep.

My heels clicked loudly on the pavement as I headed in the direction that my Jeep was parked. The area was lit, but not well. Thankfully, I wasn't afraid of the dark, and if someone tried to mug me, he'd be in for a rude surprise when I handed him his ass back.

I made it to my Jeep, grabbed my hidden key. In no time, I was in and ready to go. I grabbed my phone from the glove box and noticed the amount of missed calls I had. Scrolling through them, I saw that nearly all were from Jay. Zachariah was next in line. I accessed one from Jay.

"Dammit, Gina, answer your phone. You need to get out of the fucking club. Now."

When I got to the sixth voice mail from him, I sighed. "Gina, shit. The pack members watching the club got pulled away with an emergency. I'm coming as fast as I can."

The rest of the messages from him were a lot of the same. At some point, he'd gone from seeming as if he saw me as a competent slayer, to acting like it was my first week out of training. On the one hand it felt nice to know someone cared, but on the other, it was slightly insulting.

I pulled out of the parking lot and headed in the direction of home, having no intention of going to Zachariah's for the night. What Jay didn't know wouldn't hurt him. Besides, he wasn't my keeper.

I made it another three blocks from the club when a tire blew. Several curses later, I was out of the Jeep and surveying the damage. The tire was toast. There was no saving it. The last thing I wanted to do was change a tire in a dress and heels. Not to mention doimg so in the warehouse district at this time of night. It was always a favorite stomping ground for supernaturals looking to have some fun without repercussions. Having to kick some demon ass while in four-inch heels and a dress that just barely covered my breasts wasn't high on my bucket list.

As I soaked in what was around me, I couldn't help but notice the vast amounts of graffiti on the majority of the warehouses and office buildings. This stretch of the warehouse district managed to be more run-down than others. I suspected it was due to the fact most of the businesses that operated out of this portion had gone belly-up at some point. Not a surprise with the state of things.

Some of the graffiti was from humans, but a large portion was from supernaturals. It was easy to tell the difference. The symbols and tags used were different. I'd learned all the local supernatural tags some time ago. Many just announced that the area was part of a supernaturals' territory, or turf if we were taking it back to '80s movie time. Others were warnings to humans that if they entered, they wouldn't leave. Which I found ironic, since humans weren't hip to the fact supernaturals were even real.

Not sure the warning system was well-planned.

My phone rang, and I answered it quickly.

No sense allowing my phone's ringtone to act as a beacon to draw unwanted attention. If I was dressed for slaying, I'd have turned on my music and let it blare from my phone, daring the assholes to make a move.

"Hey, babes, is this a good time?" asked Lindsay, my best friend.

I grunted. "Sure. I'm about to change a tire in a dress that probably retails for several hundred dollars. It was one that Zachariah keeps in his giant room of women's clothing. Let's not even get into how weird that is."

"Call Jay," she said nonchalantly, as if Jay's manliness should be exploited at all times. For a second, I agreed with her. "He'll come change the tire for you."

Lindsay and I had been friends for what felt like forever. She was funny, sarcastic, and someone whom I'd clicked with instantly. But our personalities tended to differ to a point. She'd gone from blindly trusting everyone around her and laughing nonstop, to losing faith in everything and becoming jaded. Since she'd mated, more and more of the old Lindsay was shining through. She no longer kept armor around her heart.

I strongly suspected that was because she no longer had to live in constant fear of being attacked by whatever supernatural of the week was hunting her for her mate. Now that her mate was *with* her, they all thought twice about attacking her.

That had helped to set my mind at ease when she'd told me she was moving. I'd spent so long trying to watch over her and help as much as I could that I was happy to know she'd be safe but sad to see her go. We'd spent nearly every day together before. Now that person-to-person time was spent on the phone.

"Linds, I'm capable of changing my own tire." I retrieved my jack and set about doing as much. "Still suffering from insomnia?"

She bemoaned. "Yes. I swear all I did was sleep for the first four months I was pregnant. Now I'd give anything to sleep six straight hours."

Putting her on speakerphone, I set the phone on the ground and continued with the task of changing the tire. It was less than glamorous.

"Kill anything interesting tonight?" she

asked. "I'm so bored. Let me live vicariously through you."

Snorting, I pulled the old tire off and set it aside. "No, I haven't killed anything tonight. Zachariah had me on a recon mission. It was interesting, to say the least. I'm pretty sure I was propositioned by a really scary master vampire."

"Was he at least hot?" she asked, letting me know pregnancy had not yet ruined her sense of priorities.

"Oh yeah. He was hot. But there's something more to him," I confessed. "Something that made me want to keep my distance."

"Gina, you have like no fear," she said softly. "If he wigged you out, you need to reach out to Jay. I can send Xavs or Eion. They're taking turns making me sit still."

"They worry," I said, in response to her mate and his first cousin fretting over her.

She let out a long breath. "Well, I worry about *you*. I don't like being this far from you."

"You're two hours away," I said.

"Might as well be another planet. I'm missing out on everything. I stare at the same walls all day, hoping my overprotective husband leaves the house long enough for me to go outside and take a walk—alone."

Laughing, I went to retrieve my spare tire. "Marital bliss getting on your nerves?"

"He hovers. Every time I turn around, he's there." She grunted and then grumbled.

I snorted. "He's standing there now, isn't he?"

"Yes."

"Run, Exavier," I said, knowing his sensitive wolf-shifter hearing would pick up on my side of the conversation with ease. "She's not safe to be close to."

He chuckled. "I know. I'm thinking of wearing a cup around her."

"Just a few more months and then you'll have a little bundle of joy," I added.

"I cannot wait!" he thundered. "I want like ten more."

Lindsay sounded as if she might inflict serious bodily harm on him.

"Exavier, you might want to bring that up again after the first one comes."

"Ouch!" he said, yelping. "Okay. Let go. Baby, do not twist it off me. If you do, how am I going to handle your *other* cravings?"

"Too much information here, folks," I said, trying to get the spare on.

Lindsay laughed. "I miss you. Come stay with us for a bit."

"Can't. Lots of weird stuff has been happening around here," I said as the hair on the back of my neck rose.

It was all the warning I had before something grabbed me by the hair from behind. I dropped the tire but grabbed the tire iron. It scraped across the ground on my way up.

"S-Slayer," something said in my ear, holding me off the ground.

I didn't wait to figure out who or what it was. I acted fast, ramming the tire iron into its stomach. It dropped me and hissed.

Turning, I found the three vampires who had tried to listen in on Jay and me at the club. They weren't alone. They'd brought a number of friends.

"Gina?" asked Lindsay, the phone still on the ground by the blown tire. "What's happening?"

"Just another day in the life of me," I said, watching the men, wondering who would attack first.

It didn't take long before I got my answer. Two came at me at once. I spun and hit one with the tire iron and the other, I kicked back from me.

"Bitch!" one spat. "I will tear you to bits."

"Blah, blah, blah," I said, rolling my eyes, having heard just about every curse word out there in my line of work. Hell, I knew obscenities from hundreds of years ago, as a large part of the job left me facing off against men and women who had been alive a long, long time.

They all came at me this time. Perhaps mocking wasn't the best plan I'd had.

Live and learn.

I unleashed hell on them, ducking, weaving, just missing taking dagger-like nails to the face and neck. I kicked, hit, and bashed them with the tire iron, deflecting their blows with relative ease.

One got a good hit on me, and I went airborne before hitting the ground by the tire and phone. It didn't feel great. Not that anyone would assume it would. The tire iron skidded across the ground, just out of my reach.

"Gina!" shouted Lindsay. "Are you okay?"

The vampires used the moment to try to

gain the advantage on me. If they thought I was weaponless, they were wrong. I yanked off my heels and popped to my feet as if I had springs on my ass. Whirling around, I rammed a heel into a vampire's chest. He burst into a cloud of dust instantly. I did the same to another. He lingered a bit before turning to ash.

When a third fanger charged me, I groaned. "Really? It went so well for the first two. You looking to be the encore? You're like lemmings."

That only served to piss the rest of them off more.

One of them went up and over me, grabbed me by my hair, yanking me off the ground, causing me to drop one of my heels. I grasped his wrist, squeezing hard, knowing I was crushing his bones. He released me, and I impaled him with my remaining heel. Vamp dust rained down on me as I bent and snatched my other heel from the ground.

In the next breath, I leaped up and onto the hood of my Jeep, to get a better vantage point. When I looked up, I found there were even more of them. "You're like bunnies! You just keep multiplying."

"Xavs, call Jay! Hurry! Tell him Gina needs help," yelled Lindsay, sounding very panicked.

"Ah, this is nothing, Linds," I said, leaping off my Jeep and onto another vampire, dusting him quickly too.

Who would have thought heels would come in handy while killing supernaturals?

Stepping to the right, I watched a vampire fall into the side of my Jeep. I rammed a heel into his back, dusting him quickly as well. I kept going, fighting in the street, by myself, barefoot and in a dress that didn't exactly want to stay put while I maneuvered.

"Gina?" Lindsay asked, her voice holding concern. Then, "Exavier, what do you mean he's not answering? Screw voice mail! Can't you like zap him? You're all powerful or something, aren't you? What do you mean you're not? You're always making yourself out to be. Dammit, Xavs, I will rip pieces of you off if she gets hurt!"

Poor Exavier was going to catch hell for weeks to come over this all. I felt bad for him. Lindsay's hormones were no joke. She had the magik and the temper to make his life very difficult.

"Lindsay, stop. I'm fine," I said in between ramming my heels into more vampires. It was almost assembly line-like.

They line up.

I kill them.

I bounced a vampire's head off the hood of my Jeep. One of them clawed my back open. I winced and then spun to glare at the culprit.

He paled, which was impressive, considering he was the whitest damn vampire I'd ever seen.

Going at him extra hard, I beat him backwards before jabbing one heel into his neck and the other through his heart. I then stared down at his ashes. "Asshole."

I stood there, barefoot, in a fighting stance, breathing hard, blood dripping down my back, expecting to find more vampires to kill.

There were none.

Lindsay was still shouting at me. Apparently, she and Jay subscribed to the same panic and general loss of trust in my abilities.

Exhaling, I bent for my phone and lifted it a little slower than I usually would since I was injured. "Stop freaking out, Lindsay. I'm fine, and they're all dead or gone. See what you're missing out on here?"

She cried to the point I felt bad for her.

"Linds, I swear to you, I'm fine. I'm going to finish changing this tire and then head home. Stop trying to make Exavier come for me. I know that's what you're doing," I said with a grunt.

"You sure you're good?" asked Exavier from the background. "Eion and I are getting ready to head to you."

My life wasn't that bad if hot hunks were at the ready to rush to me, thinking I needed help when I didn't. They'd be to me quickly because they'd travel by way of magik. Not car. "I swear. Now, take your woman to bed and show her why she needs to leave your man parts intact."

He laughed. "Call if you need anything. I'm going to try to pry the phone from Lindsay's hand. Wish me luck."

Laughing, I hung up and looked around at all the ashes. That was a hell of a workout. On top of it all, I still hadn't finished changing my tire. So far tonight, I'd shown up at a vampire den that I wasn't aware was a den, had a really old, really hot master vampire offer to give me endless pleasure, my friend showed up growling like a damn fool before I basically gave him a lap dance, vamps attacked me, and now a friggin' flat tire.

Could it get any worse?

5

I LOOKED AROUND THE AREA, MAKING EXTRA sure all the baddies were gone or dust. The idea of leaving one of them to possibly hurt an innocent didn't sit well with me.

On the surface, everything in the desolate area seemed quiet now that the vampires were no longer a threat. Yet I couldn't shake the feeling that this was merely the eye of the storm.

The same darkness I'd felt in the club that had emanated from Reynaud trickled over me at such a slow rate that I nearly missed it. Had I not been focused on figuring out what else was out there, I might not have even noticed it.

His men had been the ones who'd attacked me. They'd called me a slayer the minute they'd cornered me. That meant Reynaud knew the truth about me. He knew I wasn't some random human who'd met up with her boyfriend at his club. A sinking feeling came over me when I realized he'd probably known all along what I was.

And now he was toying with me.

Turns out, the night *could* actually get worse.

My attention was pulled to my right.

Reynaud was there, leaning casually against the exterior of a building not that far from me. If darkness didn't leak from the man, I'd have thought he looked hot there. Posed as if he were doing a magazine spread. But his exterior was a ruse, something to hide the darkness in him.

Reynaud's tongue ran over his lower lip as his blue-gray gaze drew up and down me painfully slow. Everywhere his gaze went, so did raw power. It felt as if it was swallowing up the air around me, rushing over my body. The darkness enveloped me, making my head feel fuzzy, as if I'd had too much to drink. The need to make contact with the vampire was all-consuming and the next thing I knew, I was putting my hand out to him.

Hello, body. Beckoning the big scary vamp dude to you is a really stupid idea.

My body didn't seem to agree. Especially when I crooked my finger, in his direction, as if my next step was taking him to bed with me.

So not the next step.

Desire coursed through me.

Shit, it's the next step.

When the realization of what I was about to do came over me, I paused. He was successfully swaying my thoughts with his vamp mojo. And if I didn't do something to change the situation, I very well might find myself in bed with the man. After that, I'd end up a meal. Neither sounded great to me.

My mind scrambled with ways to block his control over me. Attacking him sounded great; unfortunately, whatever he was doing to me kept me from moving. Kicking his ass would be difficult if I was basically a hormonal statue, begging to be with him. I needed a tinfoil hat and a crossbow.

Of which I had neither.

I had a tire iron that I couldn't get to, and my pumps, which would be as effective on the master vampire as hitting him with a fly swatter.

I was totally—and soon to be literally—fucked.

The expression on his face said he knew as much. He was in charge of the situation. The next move was his. I was merely an unwilling pawn in his game. One that he'd just proven couldn't harm him.

I blinked, and he was in front of me, making me gasp because that never happened to me. I always saw vampires moving, knew what they were doing and felt them.

But not him.

His hold on me lessened enough for me to move. I seized the moment, trying to hit him, but he caught my hand. He didn't hurt me. He merely held my hand in his, his gaze still searching mine. I wasn't sure what he was looking for, and I didn't care. I just wanted to get away from him. As I attempted to kick him, he blocked the move, looking amused and turned on.

Trust me to find the one vampire who got horny when bodily harm was threatened.

"Gina," he said, his deep voice sliding over me.

I moaned as need slammed into me. I knew it was his doing, not my own feelings or desires.

Kill him, don't drool over him.

His soft laugh eased up my body.

My gaze hardened. "Stop."

"Gina, I could release you fully, but you will do your best to kill me, and I will be forced to attempt to cage my demon, so it would do you no real harm," he returned as if he was doing me a great big favor by taking my free will. "I want you. You will grow to want me in return."

Defiance shone brightly from me. Like hell I would. I'm pretty sure I'd stake him in his sleep.

He grinned, showing fang. "You desired the male you were with at the club. I could smell it on you. Smell the lust coming from you both. That same lust for him will happen with me in time. The sooner you stop fighting the pull, the better. I've waited a long time for you, and have spent years searching for you. I will not let another moment pass us by."

My brow quirked. "Looking for me? Why?"

"Fate," he replied, as if that one word summed up everything nicely and tied it in a bow.

I shook my head slightly and made another move to attack him.

He caught me and dragged me against his authoritative frame, his power pushing through me once more. I thought for sure I'd pant like a dog in heat. Thankfully, I didn't.

"Join me at the club and allow me to show you pleasure the likes of which you have never seen."

"Are you planning to kill me or screw me?" I asked.

"I'd much prefer the latter, but should we not find common ground, the former will occur," said Reynaud, before he took my hand in his and lifted it to his mouth, kissing the back, his long dark hair falling forward. "I was not finished with our time together, and I did not like seeing you with the other man."

"So, you sent a bunch of your men after me to be sure I got the message?"

He shrugged. "I needed to see if what I suspected was true. If you were as good as you are rumored to be."

I wasn't feeling very awesome at the moment, considering he had ahold of me and seemed to know my moves before I made them. "And?"

"I am not disappointed." He smiled. "Come, I promised you a night of pleasure."

My gaze went to the piles of ashes surrounding us.

He laughed, and the sound eased over me. I knew he was influencing me, but I didn't know how. I should have been immune to his gifts.

Apparently, I wasn't.

"Gina, I have more where they came from," he said, his gaze moving to the ashes as well.

I tensed. "Aren't you going to try to kill me?"

He touched my cheek. "No. This is where I take you back to the club, spend time with you before I take you to my bed."

His power eased over me.

I took a step back and slipped on the ashes with my bare feet.

He caught me, steadying me, his face close to mine. His free hand came to my neck. I knew I shouldn't let him near such a vulnerable spot, but I couldn't help myself. The urge to panic didn't come, and I knew he was the one keeping me from freaking out.

He stroked my neck more, keeping me bent back as he held me. "Tell me why I cannot read your thoughts. It is rare for me not to be able to read a slayer with great ease."

I stiffened. "How are you influencing me?"

His gaze raked over me. "I will admit, you are harder to control than any I've encountered before."

"Try to seduce a lot of us then?" I asked, really interested in the answer.

He waggled his brows. "No. Only one before you—my mate. The rest I tortured for months, sometimes years before finally killing them, or finding a way to convert them over to join those of us who hunt at night."

I gasped. "A slayer can't be turned into a vampire. It's not possible."

"It just takes the right vampire," he said calmly, still looking at me with an expression that freaked me out. I couldn't move to even try to get away from him. Whatever he was doing was keeping me right where he wanted me.

Boldly, he licked my neck from my collarbone to my ear. He chuckled softly. "Someone helped you to mask your natural scent."

I tensed.

He pressed his lips to my ear. "What did you come to my club for on this night? I think maybe it was *you* trying to kill *me*."

Lying was an option, but I went with the truth, kind of. "No. I didn't come to kill anyone.

I was curious about the club. I'd be remiss as a slayer if I didn't check it out."

He looked surprised by my answer, as if he was expecting a lie. With a smile, he kissed my neck, my chin, and the corner of my lips.

Try as I might, I still couldn't move.

"You are exquisite. Bedding you will be explosive," he said, sounding horny as hell. "I feel you trying to resist my hold. I have to say, you are doing so much better than any other has before you. Why is that?"

"I don't know. Maybe I just have a better sense of self-preservation," I replied, still struggling within myself to move. It was as if sleep paralysis had me in its clutches.

"Do you understand that I could take everything I wanted from you here and now?" he asked, his mouth still on the edge of my lips.

"Y-yes." My fear was real, and I knew I was shedding a tear.

He wiped it away and caressed my cheek. "I said I could. I did not say I would—yet."

"What are you?" I asked. "You're not just a vampire. Your darkness is so much more than others."

He tipped my head back more and kissed my neck gently.

As I felt his fangs break my skin, I fought with everything I had to move, to thrust him away from me, to kill him. When he started to drink from me, my need to get away from him lessened and lessened to the point it was nearly gone.

Visions of death and destruction filled my head, each one appearing as if they were my own memories. I saw a battlefield, fires, and bodies burning in all directions. The smell of the burnt flesh was nauseating. As I looked around, I smiled, knowing it was my handiwork that had caused the death, the destruction.

The vampire moved his mouth off me fast, hissing. "You were in my memories. How?"

I knew blood was trickling down me, but there was nothing I could do about it. "I don't know. Never happened to me before."

He licked the wound on my neck and studied my face for what felt like forever. "You are far more than you appear to be."

I gulped.

He kissed my lips chastely. "I have never in all my years met a woman who could fight against my hold to the extent you are. Or one who could enter my thoughts and memories. You shall make a worthy companion."

"Do I get a vote?"

He chortled. "No, Gina. You do not."

A series of howls and growls filled the area.

Reynaud perked as a sinister grin moved across his face. "I wondered if he'd come the second I found you. He does not disappoint."

"W-who? Jay?" I asked, confused.

"Step away from the lass, asshole," said a deep voice with a heavy Scottish accent.

Reynaud held me tighter to him. "Or you will what, McKay? You will huff and puff and…"

"I'll nae tell you again, you sick son of a bitch," the man said. "Release the lass, she's nae part of this battle we've been dancing around for decades."

Reynaud eyed me, and it was easy to see the wheels of his mind spinning. He looked behind me and grinned. "Wolf, you do not even fully grasp the battle or the players."

I pushed at his chest but didn't make a ton of headway.

Snarls rent the air from behind me.

"You are powerless here, and you know as much," warned Reynaud. "Continue to posture and I will kill the woman here and now. Trust me, McKay, you do not want that."

I felt my boss approaching. He wasn't traveling by ordinary means. He was flying. I knew the second he arrived.

There were more snarls.

"Go, vampire, we do nae need more of you here," snapped McKay.

"I know not who you are, but I'm no friend of Reynaud's," said Zachariah firmly, his French accent showing as well.

Reynaud couldn't have looked happier if he tried. I suspected he wore that look while kicking puppies.

Seemed the type.

He held me in place.

"Brother, you align yourself with lowly shifters?" asked Reynaud, making me gasp.

Zachariah and Mr. Tall, Dark and Scary were brothers?

"I align myself with any who stand in opposition to you," returned Zachariah. "And we are brothers only because we share a maker. That bond does not extend to the limits you have pushed it. Release her."

"Aye, I'm with the dead guy," said McKay.

Reynaud turned with me, letting me see everyone. The very same men I'd noticed in the parking lot of the club when Jay was leading me out were there. The man with the black hair and green eyes stood next to Zachariah.

"Lass, are you injured?" the man asked.

"No," I said, unable to look away from him. "I'm pretty much just pissed."

Zachariah snorted. "Why am I not surprised?"

"Because you know me well." I stared up at Reynaud. "This whole bending me backwards bit is getting old."

Reynaud dipped his head to my neck again and bit, this time making my body ignite with desire as he did. It wasn't real, and I knew it wasn't of my doing.

Zachariah and the others shouted and tried to rush us. Power I couldn't see knocked them all backwards as Reynaud continued to feed from me.

Jay flashed in my mind, and I drew upon a resolve I wasn't aware I possessed. I screamed in anger and broke the vampire's hold on me, thrusting him away from me hard enough to send him into the very building he'd been leaning against.

He didn't look pissed.

He looked like he wanted to fuck me even more now.

He licked blood from his lips.

Zachariah was with me in an instant, shoving me behind him.

McKay and the two men with him charged Reynaud. They were nearly to him when he launched into the air and hovered for a moment. He winked at me. "Sweet dreams, little slayer. See you again very soon."

With that, he was gone.

The next thing I knew, I was going down.

6

THERE WAS SOMETHING ABOUT THE SMELL OF sawdust and sweat that did it for me. It was manly, earthy, and made my body respond. It didn't hurt that the man currently covered in sawdust had a body to die for and smelled delicious all on his own. What can I say? I'm a sucker for guys who are handy. It's a major weakness of mine. Always had been. And Jay was about as sexy as they came. Finding out he was handy only added to his hotness factor.

Not that he needed any help in that category. He had sexy in spades.

I should know, I'd spent the last six months staring at him when he wasn't looking.

I'd been spending time with him, helping him with his renovation project during our

down hours for a while now—or rather
watching him renovate while I stood around and
admired his backside. I'd had to cancel on him
three days in a row because of what had
happened with Reynaud, and I still hadn't told
Jay the truth of it all. I'd also not seen McKay
or the others since that night—just Zachariah.

At first, I assumed Zachariah would call Jay
and notify him about what had happened right
away, but he hadn't. He was worried Jay would
launch a full-scale attack against the den that
would leave innocents hurt in the crossfire. A
clash of the shifters and vampires kind of
epic thing.

Zachariah had been tight-lipped about his
history with Reynaud. Other than the fact they
shared a maker, I knew nothing more. But
Zachariah did look incredibly guilty that he'd
sent me into the club alone. He'd not known
Reynaud was even in the city, let alone affiliated
with the club and den. I'd been forced to listen
to his ranting and ravings, only understanding a
tenth of them because he kept falling into
French as he shouted. He wasn't yelling at me.
More at himself while I was stuck in the room
with him. Then again, my grasp of the French

language was nothing to write home about and he could have been ranting about a pizza for all I knew.

By the end of the ranting, Zachariah was walking back and forth in his office, lifting his hands in the air, having a one-man conversation. I caught a bit about my mate finding out and doing something crazy. I found that odd since slayers didn't have mates.

A large piece of me hated that I'd kept the truth of the attack from Jay. He'd called me later that night, worried about me and my safety. Zachariah had texted him back from my phone for me, telling him I was fine and that period cramps had started, and I planned to stay home for a few days, eat ice cream, and binge-watch girlie shows.

Watching Zachariah as he typed all that into my phone had been a highlight of my week. You'd think for an immortal vampire, he'd be past the point of being wigged out by discussing a woman's menstrual cycle. He wasn't.

I hadn't started my period, and I didn't spend the time away from Jay eating ice cream and binge-watching anything. I spent it healing, tucked safely away at the main house for the slayers in the city. The one that Zachariah lived in and had his office at. The man made me stay in a bed for days so he could keep an eye on me for any side effects from what Reynaud had done to me.

That asshole had then had the nerve to put me on leave, telling me it was too dangerous for me to be patrolling with what had happened to me.

I'd informed Jay that I was forced to take some time off, but I'd been vague about it, knowing he'd dig deeper and blow his lid.

He was protective like that.

As I watched him work, the need to tell him everything continued to press at me. I tried to keep it tamped down.

Jay had been working on the old home, restoring it room by room, for about seven months now. I wasn't sure how he actually lived there. He basically had a bed and some clothes there. Nothing else. Not that I could judge with as few items as I had in my apartment. It was a place to lay my head, nothing more.

When Jay had first asked me over to help, I really thought he'd meant to help. Unless he wanted moral support, I hadn't done anything each time I'd been there. When I'd come today, I'd foolishly thought he'd finally let me assist him. So far, he'd been steadily moving me out of his way all morning. I didn't mind. Each time he touched me, I had to hide a smile because of the tingles that raced through me. I had to remind myself more than once—okay, more than a hundred times—that it was just Jay.

Jay was a friend, and I didn't do friends.

Why the hell did I come up with that rule?

Willpower wasn't something I was over-flowing with when it came to the man anymore. At one point I had been, but as of late, I was fighting a losing battle. Damn him and his manly sweat smell with a hint of sawdust over it for dramatic effect. And damn him for being handy, lifting heavy things, and hammering.

All of it turned me on.

The urge to shove him was great, like it was his fault I couldn't control my hormones around him. It fit with my temper, but I resisted. Mostly because I wasn't sure making any type of phys-ical contact with the man was wise. I'd probably tackle him and rub myself all over him or some-thing else stupid. With my sudden lack of willpower, there was a real possibility anything would happen.

Folding my legs, I sat on the edge of the countertop, doing my best to stay out of Jay's way and keep my mouth shut about Reynaud.

Jay pushed his pencil behind his ear while he went to work measuring a board. He was quite the handyman. I stared down at him and laughed as I spotted the coating of sawdust in his black hair. He seemed to wear almost as much sawdust as the floor. The floor didn't look anything as close to good with it on as he did though.

Calm down there, girlie bits. You friend-zoned Jay long ago. Stop trying to hump his leg.

I couldn't tear my gaze from him. Stubble covered his square jawline and he stared up at me with chocolate-brown eyes. The entire package was something to behold indeed.

Sexy and able to fix things.

What more could a girl ask for?

"Gina, I'm *so* happy you agreed to help me with this project," he said, his voice deep.

"Hey, I tried to help, but you told me to move out of your way." Putting my fingers up for emphasis, I widened my eyes. "Three times."

"The best spot you could come up with to be out of the way was the countertop in the kitchen I'm remodeling?"

I took a deep breath and glanced away, realizing he'd only asked me to hang with him out of pity, not because he really wanted me there. "I'll go. Sorry. I really didn't mean to be in the way."

I made a move to get off the counter, but he was over to me in a flash, his large, muscular body pinning me in place. The feel of him so close to me left me breathless.

"I don't want you to go," he said. "I was joking, Gina. I haven't seen you in three days, and you've been so quiet that I just wanted to get you talking. Even yelling at me, which you love to do. That's all. I swear."

Putting my palm to his chiseled chest, I glanced up at him, unable to look away from him as he stood there covered in sawdust, smelling yummy. "Close your eyes."

"Why?" He arched a black brow.

"Just do it."

He did, and I immediately began brushing the sawdust from his ear-length hair. I took my time, liking the feel of his hair more than I should. As he peeked out of one eye, he tipped his head.

"What are you doing?" he asked, the makings of a smile starting.

God, I did love it when the man smiled.

"Cleaning you. I wanna see those brown eyes without a layer of sawdust threatening to fall into them." I wrinkled my nose playfully as he moved closer to me. "Seriously, though. I get you feel the need to spend time with me because my friends aren't around right now, and I've effectively been benched as far as slayer duties, but you don't have to do that. I'm fine on my own."

He took a large breath, his body pressing harder against mine. He dipped his head more, his face nuzzling against my neck. He took a deep breath in and then growled lightly, grabbing my legs, uncrossing them, and then putting them to each side of his hips. Hooking an arm around my waist, he yanked me closer to him, leaving us groin to groin.

I gasped. "Jay?"

He growled again, his lips near my ear. "Don't go," he said, his voice even more profound than it usually was.

"J-Jay, what are you doing?" I asked, my voice barely there.

"Smelling you," he said, as if that wasn't the least bit weird.

I wasn't a shifter. I didn't go around sniffing people. Just then, I drew in his scent again and realized that, apparently, I did sniff people. Well, I at least sniffed Jay. A soft laugh came from me. "Don't mock me later when I say this, but you smell really good."

He nuzzled his face against my neck more. "So do you."

For a moment, I fought the urge to kiss him.

Jay growled yet again, and I felt his cock hardening in his jeans. As his erection became evident, I got a pretty good idea how big the man was.

Jay could rip a woman in two.

"Gina."

"Y-yes?" I asked with a shaky voice that I wasn't exactly proud of since it made it obvious I was affected by him too.

He inhaled again. "Why did you tell me you'd started menstruating when you hadn't? You just started to ovulate."

I yelped. "What?"

"I can smell it on you. I can always smell when your body changes," he said, his voice low.

Gasping, I jerked, only serving to push my groin to his. "Tell me you're joking."

"I'm not." He ran a hand up my back and into my long dark red hair. Tugging lightly, he forced my head back, giving him better access to my neck. If I wouldn't have known he was a wolf shifter, I'd have thought he was a vampire at the moment. Not that I'd have cared. He felt too good pushed against me.

"G-Gina," he said, sounding labored as his entire body coiled. "Push me away."

"Jay?"

His voice deepened. "Push me away. I'm struggling for control. I don't want to hurt you. Hit me, kick me. Whatever you have to do to protect yourself from me."

I slid my hands up his chest and wrapped my legs around his waist. We'd never had a moment like this before, and I wasn't exactly sure how to handle it, but I did know one thing —Jay wouldn't hurt me.

"Jayson, it's okay."

He tensed, his arms flexing. "N-not okay."

"Look at me," I said in an even tone as I began to sense his fear, his worry over harming me.

"Can't," he ground out, his voice even deeper.

"Jayson."

Unhurriedly, he lifted his head from my neck and looked at me. His brown eyes were now a vibrant amber. I knew then his wolf was beating at him from within.

I leaned in and hugged him to me. I put my head on his chest. "Stop worrying. You would never ever hurt me. I know it as sure as I know the sun will rise and set."

Slowly, the tension in him began to alleviate.

I eased back a touch and looked up to find him watching me with a curious expression on his handsome face. I smiled wide and then put my arms over his shoulders, pulling myself up and off the counter, my legs still wrapped around him.

He lifted me to him more. "Gina?"

Giggling, I leaned up and kissed him just below each eye. "Put the wolf away, Jay. Then you need to get back to sawing stuff and hammering. I have got to say, the sight of you doing that is a major turn-on. And I'm going to admit to liking the smell of sawdust. Warning, if you do keep having me around when you reno-vate, there is a high likelihood that I'm going to throw you down and have my way with you. Now, grab *your* tool and show me what you want me to do."

The amber faded back to brown as he grinned. "Hmm, have a fetish for men in construction?"

"Not *all* men." I gave him a quick squeeze and then slid out of his hold. When my feet were on the floor, I swatted his abs lightly. "Get to hammering."

"Oh, I nearly was hammering," he said, his voice suggestive. "If you want to help, you could play with my tool."

There was the Jay I knew. I laughed. "Maybe later. For now, put me to work. But if you ever talk about my period or me ovulating, I might harm you, badly."

7

He caught my hand. "Gina, I'm sorry about what just happened. I didn't mean to lose control. It's been getting harder and harder for me over the last six months."

Concern cut through me. I grabbed his hands in mine. "What's wrong? Why would you suddenly have issues controlling your shifter side?"

Averting his gaze, he stayed in place, holding my hands. "No reason."

There was a slight tug in my gut. "Jayson Louis Gonzales, if you don't tell me the truth, I'm going to take one of these two-by-fours and whap you upside the head."

He licked his lips, grinning ever so slightly.

"This is funny? You know as well as I do that things in the supernatural community have been growing worse at a rapid rate. It's like something is feeding the anger, the rage, the darkness everyone carries. If whatever is happening is starting to affect you, tell me. I'll help you somehow. I don't care what rock I have to turn over, I will find a way to make you be okay."

"Gina, I'm fine. I promise," he said, still grinning. "I don't find control issues funny. I've seen too many of my kind suffer from them. I laughed because you scolded me like I was a child and used my full name. I wasn't aware you knew it."

"Jay, you'd come to me, right?" I asked, my lips starting to tremble. "I mean, if you were having problems, you'd trust me enough to come to me, wouldn't you?"

He looked away quickly, and I took it as a sign he didn't trust me to the level I did him.

I released his hands and stepped back. "I get it. I shouldn't have pushed, and I know shifters don't trust any slayer fully. It's amazing that you and I can tolerate being around each other. Listen, thanks for letting me hang here. I'm tired. I'm going to head home."

"Stop trying to leave me," he said in a gruff voice.

Leave him?

In one step, he was to me. "Gina, I'm trying to figure out how to tell you that my control issues are with *you*. Only you. That when I'm near you, I have to be mindful of that side of myself. Christ, your smell drives me nuts all the time. This time of the month, it's as hard for me to control myself as it was when I was going through puberty and a full moon would occur. I don't want to hurt you."

Shock coursed through me. "Your wolf wants to hurt me?"

"For fuck's sake, baby, my wolf wants me to give in to my urges. It wants me to pin you and fuck you senseless. I have to tell you, the red dress at the club didn't help matters any. Neither did rubbing all over you, your breasts in my face, your legs spread open on my lap. And the change in your scent tonight pushed me over the edge."

For several seconds, no sound was made. Jay's wolf wanted to do me? I wasn't exactly sure how to respond to that.

He exhaled slowly. "I just made it super

weird between us, didn't I? I should have pinched your ass after I said it. Then you'd have hit me and all would be right in the Gina and Jay universe. You're going to start locking it down when I want to touch you, aren't you? Like you used to do to me."

I knew I could have lied and told him things would be awkward between us, so I could have an out for the way I felt about him. But blowing off the fact he'd shown vulnerability moved me. And the truth was, I felt something for him. It wasn't something I was sure I wanted to admit to anyone, including myself, but it was there all the same. I didn't let many men under my armor. Hell, I didn't let many men *or* women under it. The burning need to let him know that things had changed in my eyes was so great, that I folded.

I hooked my index finger around his. Bravely, I looked up at him. "If I tell you something, you have to swear to me that you won't laugh or belittle it."

If he did, I'd probably stake him. Didn't matter that stakes weren't used for shifters. Wood was all around me, so it was all I had.

He nodded.

I wavered, unsure I actually wanted to admit to him what I had a hard time acknowledging myself.

"Gina?"

I wet my lips. "I've been having some issues over the past six months, too."

"Who hurt you? I'll rip their fucking heads off," he said, growling again, sounding like he was on the verge of shifting.

"Jayson, stop." I tightened my finger around his. "My issues have been when I'm around *you*."

He stilled, his gaze cautious. "What do you mean?"

Laying myself bare before him wasn't exactly easy for me. "It's hard to explain. Before, the idea of you with other women was funny to me. All the teasing about you wanting to touch me and trying to get me to sleep with you was funny, and honestly a bit annoying sometimes."

He closed his eyes.

"Jay…that's kind of changed. I don't know why, and I really don't want to dig deeper into it right now." I looked away, already totally understanding what the shift in views meant. But I couldn't confess it out loud just yet. I wasn't ready. "I swear if you mock this or try to proposition me with a lame come-on, I will beat you to the brink of death."

He tugged me closer to him. "Talk to me, Gina. I'm here and listening. Tell me what exactly changed and when."

Nodding, I looked at the floor. "About six months ago, it started to really bother me when the girls and I would talk, and one of them would bring up one of the many, many, *many* chicks you've banged. It, um…well, it hurt to hear about you with other women. I don't know why. It's why I asked you not to text me and give me details about you and your conquests."

He touched my chin, and when I looked up, I saw his brown eyes were moist. "If I could go back in time and change things, I would. I didn't know then. I swear to you. Had I known, everything would be different. You're going to think this is a bullshit line coming from me, but it's the truth."

"Jay, you didn't know what?" I asked, remembering him saying the same thing to me in his SUV.

"Gina, I don't think you're ready for me to tell you everything."

I wouldn't be able to handle details of his time with other women.

"Can we maybe not talk about this anymore right now? I don't want to feel awkward around you," I said, needing to get off the subject before I blurted out things I couldn't take back. "Though, the idea you can smell me ovulating is still super awkward. Have you always been able to do that?"

He nodded.

I swatted him.

Laughing, he waggled his brows and winked. "Want me to offer to nail you while I'm hammering? Would that help to ease the fact I can smell that you're ripe and it's turning me on?"

Laughter escaped me, and the trepidation I'd felt letting him under my armor a little passed at once. "There's the Jay I know and love. Let me really help here."

"All right." He guided me over to the sawhorses. He measured out something on the piece of wood there and marked it with a pencil before easing me in front of him, supporting the wood with one hand while he pressed his front against my back. Almost instantly I felt his body heat, and mine began to do the same. "Shit. This is a bad idea."

"Because you're worried you'll get another hard-on?" I asked, glancing over my shoulder at him with a playful look on my face.

Jay reached down between us and adjusted himself. "All-the-time problem around you anymore."

"I noticed when I was on the counter. And let me be the first to say, impressive. Very impressive."

His deep laugh rolled over me as he used his other hand to pick up the saw. "Hold on. I need to get something. Don't cut your arm off in the meantime."

"Ha, ha." I watched as he grabbed protective eyewear that I hadn't seen him bother once with when he was sawing things. He eased them onto my face and pushed my hair over my shoulders.

The glasses instantly slid down my nose and off. I caught them and put them on again, only to have the same thing happen. Grunting, I put them on and tipped my head back, in an attempt to keep them on. It didn't exactly work. "Christ, Jay, how big are you?"

"Pretty sure we've already established that," he said with a wink.

I handed him the glasses. "These aren't going to stay up on me."

Hesitating, he looked at the saw and then me. He paled.

I leaned into him, my hand finding his arm. "You look sick at the idea of teaching me how to do this."

"I kind of am," he admitted. "What if you cut your hand off? What if you drop it and the safety fails, and it slices you wide open? What if wood shavings fly into your green eyes? What if you slip and fall, and a nail gun is close and plugged in and it goes off, nailing you in the head or something?"

It was easy to see he was spooling. I put my hands on his large shoulders and couldn't find it in me to scold him for thinking I was some shrinking violet. It was sweet that he cared that much. And that meant something to me.

"Jay, if you're uneasy having me around the power tools, I can do something else. I could paint the extra upstairs bedroom that you finished last week, if you want," I offered.

He seemed to think about it before nodding. "That sounds good. Let me clean up here and I'll help."

Rolling my eyes, I snorted. "You don't trust me enough to paint unsupervised. Afraid I'll slip and impale myself with a paintbrush?"

"Maybe I just like being around you and don't want to miss out on time with you." He took my hand in his. "Let's paint."

He led me through his home, up the stairs and to one of the extra rooms. It didn't take long before we were up and running.

I stood on the ladder and edged along the ceiling as Jay used the roller. As I got into the groove of it all, I began to hum and rock slightly on the ladder. After a few minutes, my ass began to heat. Turning, I found Jay totally and completely focused on my ass.

"Uh, Jay?"

His gaze snapped up to my face. He had the decency to blush.

I laughed. "Look your fill?"

"No. Turn around so I can look some more," he said suggestively.

I smiled and got down to refill the paint holder I was using.

"Gina, what language was that song you were singing in?" he questioned.

I paused. "I'm not exactly sure. I've known it forever and a day. It's something my father used to sing to me when I was little."

He didn't look away from me. "I didn't know you could sing."

Uncomfortable, I bit my inner cheek. "I like the color you picked for in here."

"Want to go with me later in the week to pick out more colors for the other rooms?" He put the roller in the pan of paint. "We could make a date of it. Maybe grab some food, do whatever you want for a while and then pick out paint colors for the rest of the house."

"You have got to be sick of me," I stressed. "I'm a lot, and now that I'm benched from slayer duties, I'm here on your nights off, too. I'm about to save time and make you give me a key and let me have a drawer, since I'm nearly living here as it is."

He eased closer to me and bent, his face near mine. "I'll have a key ready for you tomorrow morning. You can have as many drawers as you want."

The idea was hysterical. "Okay. In no way would I annoy the hell out of you."

"I missed having you around the last few days," he said. "But I'm not sure why you lied to me about why you didn't want me around. You could have just said you wanted time away from me."

My throat tightened. "Jay, that wasn't it. I *did* want you around."

"Then why lie?"

I swallowed hard. "I can't talk about it. Zachariah's orders. Please respect that."

He was quiet for a moment before pressing a smile to his handsome face.

"How about we take a break," he said, crowding his body to mine.

That was fine by me. I liked the feel of him.

"Let's go grab something to eat. Sound good?" he asked.

I glanced down at myself, noting the fact I was in a pair of cut-off shorts, a white shirt, and a plaid, long-sleeved shirt that was made for a woman but mimicked a man's. Not to mention I had on a pair of bright blue Chucks.

"Uh, Jay, you don't want to be seen with me like this."

He laughed. "I think you look gorgeous. Let me get a helmet for you and we can go grab some food."

I always liked riding on his motorcycle with him. It hadn't happened a lot, but the few times it did, I liked being able to wrap my arms around his waist. "Sounds like a plan."

We wrapped up the paint and brushes before heading back downstairs.

He hurried off, and when he came back, he had a black helmet that looked like it would never in a million years fit him. It had flames on the sides. As he handed it to me, I noticed the back of it had *Fiery One* painted on it. That was what he tended to call me at random times.

"Jay?"

"Don't overthink it," he said. "Just put it on."

I did, and he helped with the strap.

He then took my hand in his and led me out of the back door to his bike. My white Jeep was parked next to it. Jay threw a long, powerful leg over the bike and straddled it before putting his hand out to me. He guided me onto the seat behind him. I put my feet where he'd taught me to put them and then slid my arms around his waist.

Jay caressed me before he turned the bike on. "Hold on, baby."

I did.

8

I SAT LOTUS STYLE ON THE CITY BENCH, FACING Jay. The night was beautiful so sitting outside worked out well. We'd ended up downtown, at a hot dog vendor that was open all night. It was one I stopped by on a regular basis because my work hours were nearly always night shift. The vendor was across the street from a park I enjoyed patrolling. The park had various iron sculptures throughout from local artists. Not to mention a beautiful fountain in the center.

"I could do this every night," I said dreamily.

Jay laughed. "Get hot dogs?"

"Hey, these are great hot dogs. Did you miss the fact I ate three?" I asked with a smile.

Jay eyed me. "You're a tiny slip of a woman. Where the hell do you put all the food you eat?"

"That was nothing. I once ate seven hot dogs in twenty minutes. Myra got sick watching me do it. I love food. I wish I could cook. Though, if I could, I might not leave the house. I'd just eat and eat."

He laughed and took a sip of his soda. "I thought I knew you well," he said. "But over the last several months, it seems like I learn something new about you all the time."

"I'm a woman of mystery," I said, chuckling as I sipped my soda. "Unless we're discussing my menstrual cycle, and then I'm apparently an open book."

Jay laughed. "I should have kept that to myself."

"Ya think?" I countered.

He put his large hand on my knee. "Gina, can I ask why Zachariah is making you sit on the bench, especially with everything going on in the city, and hell, all over? Seems like this is the time he'd want you on around the clock. I know for a fact you're the best slayer he has in this area. And I'd like to ask that you be truthful with me."

Zachariah had warned me against telling Jay the truth, but I couldn't outright lie to him. "I'm not in trouble or anything. And I have a lot of vacation time built up. Like fourteen weeks' worth."

That was true. I did have fourteen weeks of vacation built up. I wasn't using my vacation time while on paid leave, but it was true that I had it.

He lifted a brow. "Fourteen weeks? Do you ever stop working and take a break?"

"No," I said flatly before sipping my soda. "I mean, sometimes I have to miss a day or two if I end up in the med unit, but I don't take personal time or vacations. Why would I? I don't have anyone to spend the time with. I do my job and help at the rec center. That's pretty much my life."

He squeezed my knee. "I bet your parents miss you. You could fly back and spend time with them."

I licked my lips and waited a few seconds before I spoke. "Jay, they kind of stopped asking me to come home when I turned eighteen and went off to college. They offered me money to travel if I wanted to over summer and winter breaks, but um, they prefer I not come home."

He sat up more. "Why?"

I teared up but smiled wide, trying to cover it. "Wake up one day the summer before your freshman year in high school, turn into a supernatural killing machine, and everyone is suddenly freaked out by you. Win some. Lose some."

"Afraid of you?" he asked, looking perplexed. "How can they be afraid of you? One of them has to be a supernatural, too. You know how it works."

I sipped my soda. "Neither of them is supernatural."

"Gina, that can't be right."

I put my hand over his on my knee. "Jayson, they're not my biological parents."

He tipped his head. "I didn't know you were adopted. Do Lindsay and Myra know?"

"Lindsay's known since we met. Myra learned later."

"You don't like talking about it," Jay stated. "I'm sorry I pushed you for answers."

"It's fine, really. But imagine being them and adopting this child you thought was the perfect fit for your life, only to have her wake up one day and be more than human."

He grunted. "Why are they afraid of you? Sure, you can kick ass, but you'd never hurt them."

He rubbed my knee.

"When Lindsay and her father sat my parents down to explain what I was, which didn't happen until about seven months after I came into my gifts, they looked horrified. And they couldn't wrap their minds around it all. They pretty much heard I was born to kill and that was it. Then they heard monsters were real. That really drove home what they'd gotten themselves into.

"It's cool though, because I had so many freedoms after that. Spent a ton of time at Lindsay's. Her parents never judged me. Instead, her father would joke about me controlling any urges I might have with wanting to stake him because his wife really disliked dust."

Jay's jaw was tight.

"Before I left for college, my parents put extra locks on their bedroom door. Soon after, they had all the locks changed, so my key no longer worked to open the house doors. When I came and went, one of them would let me in."

"What about any other family members? Are they scared of you too?" he asked, looking as if he wanted to hit something on my behalf.

It was a kind thought, but I'd come to terms with how that part of my life had played out and didn't hold any hard feelings against them. I'd tried to put myself in their shoes, and I could understand, to a degree, where they were coming from. They hadn't signed up for the supernatural, and they were only human.

"I don't have any other family. I mean, my biological father might still be alive somewhere, but I wouldn't know him if he was standing before me. So no one. Unless you count Lindsay and Myra. Other than that, there isn't anyone else. Maybe Zachariah, but that's it." I glanced away. "And you. You sort of feel like family to me in a way."

"Gina." The way he looked at me spoke volumes. He felt bad for me.

I didn't need that.

"I don't blame my parents. They were really good to me until I came into my gifts. They had no idea supernaturals were real, let alone their daughter was one. I haven't actually talked to them at all in months. When I do, the conversation is about two minutes long. I tell them I'm alive and they say be careful and then hang up."

"You know, if you married me, you'd have a huge fucking family. So many people around you that you'd be happy for alone time," he said, patting my knee.

Sadness settled over me. "I'm good. The only time it bothers me is around the holidays. Myra goes to her mom's. Lindsay goes to see her parents, and now I'm sure Exavier's parents as well. I go nowhere, and the few people I've let close to me are gone. I take extra shifts at work, so others can spend time with their families, and I volunteer at the soup kitchen over on Ninth Street. I've learned to be alone a lot, but it's hard around holidays."

"Next holiday, you'll be spending it with me. Before you protest, know that I can cook, and I have no problem throwing you over my shoulder and taking you with me." He leaned close, his expression suggestive.

"Okay, but only if you help at the soup kitchen with me." I squeezed his hand on my knee.

"Deal." He went from touching my knee to holding my hand. "Now, I want to know more about this forced leave. Zachariah didn't say why he was forcing you to take it?"

I swallowed hard. "Jay, if I asked you to leave this alone, would you?"

"Is it about your safety?"

I nodded.

"I want to respect your wishes and let it be, but if it's about your safety, I can't," he said, no malice in his voice. "What did he say?"

"He said it was too dangerous for me to be on patrol right now. And something about my mate finding out what had happened and going crazy. But he said that in French, so I only caught bits and pieces of it," I said, telling him some but omitting other parts. "All of the ranting was ridiculous. Slayers don't have mates. They find a guy and fall in love the normal way."

He slid me closer to him with one pull. "Did he hint at who your mate was?"

"Jay, I just got done telling you I can't possibly have one."

"Humor me, Gina." He lifted me like a

child and set me on his lap. "What else did he say about this mate?"

"I really don't know. I've picked up on some French over the years working for him. But he was pretty worked up. He moved in and out of French to start with, going on and on about how *you'd* launch an attack against someone, and there would be chaos, then he paced around his office, moving to all French, talking about how he'd have to answer to my mate for this, and that my mate would go crazy over it." That was as close to the truth as I wanted to get.

Zachariah was right.

Jay would totally lose his shit and attack the den.

Jay kept me close. "He talked about your mate and me in the same rant?"

I nodded and shrugged. "I really need to learn more French, because from what I could gather, he was getting you and my mate confused. A lot. But that can't be right. I suck at French."

Jay squeezed me gently. "Have you ever given any thought to who your mate might be? Assuming, of course, you had one."

I took a deep breath. "I never thought about

it until Zachariah's endless ranting. I was trapped with it for three full days. At one point, I actually tried to concentrate on who my supposed mate might be if Zachariah was right. All I could come up with was the guy I was with for my first three years of college, but that didn't feel right. Plus, I couldn't stop thinking about you."

He stiffened. "Gina, you were with a guy for three years?"

I nodded.

"Give me his name," he growled out.

"Sam." I tucked myself against Jay's frame. "It's not a big deal. Things didn't work out. I'm over it now. Now I just use men for sex. No fuss. No muss."

"Talking about being with other men will leave me fighting to stay in control of myself, Gina. I don't like hearing about it," he said evenly.

"You asked, and I don't like hearing about all your conquests. I've either met or know how many of them?" I gave him a pointed stare.

Suddenly, he looked like he no longer wanted to have this conversation. I could still sense his underlying tension.

9

JAY KEPT ME ON HIS LAP ON THE CITY BENCH. "Gina, what happened that Zachariah didn't want me finding out about?"

The ringing of his phone saved me from having to respond.

Lucky me.

Jay yanked me against him to the point I grunted, and he answered the phone. From the sound of his side of the conversation, it was a work call. "Can't Taylor handle this? Fine. I'll come in and check it out."

I twisted into him more, my hand going to his shoulder. I didn't know Taylor, but from the sounds of it, the guy didn't do dick at work.

Jay hung up and anger rolled off him.

I sat up straight, unsure what had made his mood sour. "Jay?"

"I need to head into the station."

"Are you pissed at me?" I asked, unable to shake the feeling he might be.

"What?" he asked, pulling me against him to the point I thought I'd pop. "No. Why would you think that?"

"Because all of the sudden you're radiating a lot of anger."

He closed his eyes a second. "I didn't get to see you the last few nights. I was looking forward to spending this time with you."

I touched his face, his words moving me emotionally. "Hey, we can see each other tomorrow night—if we can find the time."

His arms wrapped around me. "That's just it. I'm sick of having to *find* time for each other. Penciling each other in doesn't work for me. I want more. Don't you?"

I wasn't sure what to say. I did want more but voicing it wasn't really my style. "Um, I should let you go. I need to head to the rec center anyway and look over applications for some new hires. Myra is freaking out about finding a replacement for Lindsay." I shrugged.

"I never knew it would be so hard to find someone to dance around a pole. It's not that far. I can walk so you can head straight to the department."

Jay's face hardened, and I instantly felt bad for bringing up Lindsay's name. I know he'd told me it had been just sex between them, but from the looks of it, my first instinct had been right. I pushed up and out of his arms. Standing, I tugged my shorts down a little and then cleaned up our hot dog mess, putting it in a trash can near us.

I didn't think it was possible for his expression to harden anymore. I was wrong. For a split second, I was sure I'd heard his teeth gritting.

I shouldn't have brought up Lindsay again. I knew that.

And despite all his claims about his time with her meaning very little, his behavior said that wasn't the case.

"Fine," he bit out. "If you didn't want to be *with me*, all you had to do was tell me so."

Flabbergasted, I blinked several times before shaking my head. "Jay, I never once said I didn't want to—"

He went in the direction of his bike with a

scowl on his gorgeous face, mumbling something along the way. The strangest part of it all
was how very much I wanted to run after him,
soothe his temper, and assure him we were okay.

There is no us.

"Sure. You get called into work, and I'm the
bad guy for stepping back so you can go in." I
started in the opposite direction and then
paused. The need to look at him was great, so
I did.

Jay had his head bent, leaning one arm
against a light pole. As jealous as I was, thinking
about his time with Lindsay and a string of
other women, I didn't have it in me to leave him
in this state.

"Jay?"

He ignored me.

"Jayson," I said, as he moved a bit, keeping
his head bent. "If you, umm, need to talk or
anything, you know where to find me."

Being "there" for people didn't come naturally to me. I tended to prefer to punch my
problems out of my system. Myra had been
working with me on expressing my anger in a
productive manner. Silly me, I sort of thought
pummeling the bad guys into a bloody pulp was

productive. Since I was new to being a pillar of support, I wasn't sure what to do.

"I can only imagine how hard it is for you to see Lindsay with Exavier now. And I know you keep telling me you're not still into her. But the minute I brought up her name again, I get you pouting and being pissy with me. If it's any consolation, I kind of know what it feels like to lose someone you care about." Where was a demon when I needed one? Staking something would make me feel much better. "Anyway, I'm here if you need a shoulder or anything. Okay?"

He turned his head and stared back at me through narrowed eyes. "You think I'm pissed because you brought up Lindsay?"

Yeah almost fell out of my mouth. I held back.

He didn't wait for my response. "I'm not, but you refuse to get that. Gina, I'm pissed that its clear you don't share my feelings for *you*."

I tipped my head. "What do you mean?"

He snorted. "I tell you I want more from you and you respond with telling me you're headed to the rec center. Pretty fucking clear you were avoiding answering me because you don't share my feelings."

I lowered my gaze.

He huffed. "See."

"Jay, did you ever think that I don't know how to handle any of this? That it's overwhelming? That I'm doing the best I can with it all? And that, maybe, just maybe, you're reading me wrong?"

My cell phone rang, and the minute I heard the "Monster Mash" ringtone, I knew it was slayer headquarters phoning me. I answered. "Gina here."

"Gina," said Zachariah, sounding winded. "Where are you? Are you okay?"

"I'm having yet another argument with Jay," I said, glancing at Jay. Something was wrong. "What's going on?"

"We just discovered the bodies of four of our own," said Zachariah, his voice tight.

"Four slayers are dead?"

"Gina, I've issued a Code Blue. We're trying to locate the rest of you. Lucy's and Tabitha's phones aren't giving us a GPS location."

I tensed. "I'll check this area and go to all the normal hot spots for baddies."

"No!" shouted Zachariah. "You are to

remain with Jay. The rest of us will handle locating Lucy and Tabitha."

"Something is out there hunting slayers, and you want me to stay with Jay?" I asked, my temper rising. "No way in hell are you keeping me benched."

"I can, and I am," said Zachariah. "You need to keep a leash on him during this. You know how Jay is. He'll want you close and safe."

Sighing, I lowered my gaze. "Please don't keep me out of the loop on this. Tell me who's dead."

"It's not a concern for you right now," he said in a scarily calm voice. "Stay with Detective Gonzales. And keep me abreast of your location."

He hung up.

Code Blue in the world of slayers meant one of us had fallen and the rest of us were required to disclose our locations so Zachariah had a lock on us, to assure we were safe.

I put my phone in my back pocket, mentally ran down the list of slayers I knew were in the area and working this weekend. Since I was on forced leave, someone would be covering my spot. I just didn't know who. And while I didn't feel totally accepted by them, I didn't want any of them hurt.

"Gina," Jay said, so close behind me that I jolted. I hadn't heard him move. He ran his hands over my shoulders. "Talk to me, baby."

"Slayer Code Blue," I whispered. "Four are down and confirmed dead. Two are missing."

Jay had me spun around and in his arms before I knew what was going on. I sank into his steely body, pressing my head to his chest and inhaling his masculine scent.

"Who is dead?"

I shook my head. "I don't know. And Zachariah is refusing to tell me. He's also forbidden me from helping with what's going on. I know he's scared about what happened the other night, but to keep me benched during this is wrong."

He wisely left my comment alone, choosing instead to rub my shoulders.

"I'm going to take the world's longest walk to the rec center and try to find out anything I can about what's happening. You're needed at the station. Go. I'll text you when I get to the rec center."

"No." Jay rubbed tiny circles on the back of

my neck, making my body heat with need. "I'll call and tell them I can't make it."

"Jay." I clung to him. "You have to go in. You know you do. I'll be fine. I'll call Myra and—"

"Myra's visiting her mother still. Remember?" He led me to his bike. "Come on."

"What?"

"I'm not leaving you alone. I can't believe I was even going to let you walk away. Your fucking boss put you on the bench because you're in danger and I let anger outweigh my better judgment. No. You're not leaving my sight." He kissed my forehead. "We'll stop by the station, and we might be able to find out what happened with the slayers. You can glance through reports in my office to see if any names or descriptions stick out."

Emotions I couldn't explain surged through me. The next thing I knew, I had my arms around Jay's neck, squeezing him tight and pressing my lips to his cheek, my feet dangling off the ground.

"Thank you." I kissed his cheek again. "Thank you." I moved to kiss the other cheek, and he turned his head. Our lips collided, and I almost slipped him the tongue.

"Thank you," I whispered against his full lips.

Jay lifted me higher off the ground and stood tall. I couldn't help but laugh. He chuckled too. "I need to make you a step stool. You're just a little bit, aren't you?"

"I only need the stool if I'm trying to reach you, so unless you plan on kissing me all the time, you can save your carpentry skills for the kitchen."

He put his forehead on mine. "So, what you're saying is, I need to start on the stool the minute we get back to the house?"

"Yes," I said softly, staring at his lips. I shook my head. "I mean, no. Jay!"

He winked and set me down. "Let's go."

10

Jay pulled his motorcycle to a stop in his designated parking space, and I climbed off quickly. I put the helmet where he had when we were eating and watched as he slid off the bike with liquid hotness.

My body tightened.

"Come on, baby," he said, putting his hand out to me. "Let's see what we can dig up."

I took his hand.

When we got to the entrance, I opened the door before he could.

He gave me a pointed look. "You make it hard to be a gentleman."

I snorted. "Considering it's you I'm with right now, gentleman never came to mind."

It was his turn to laugh. He put his hand on

the small of my back and led me through the station's front door. A thin man, only an inch or so taller than me, stepped out first. He wore a tan shirt and had a notepad in his hand. Jay groaned as he spotted the man.

"Detective Gonzales, are you here for the murder case?" the man asked. "Have anything to say about the recent uptick in violent crimes in the city?"

Jay towered over him and gave him a hard look. "What have I told you, Wilford?"

The man gulped. I'd be nervous too with someone the size of Jay in my face like that. "Umm, not to speak to you—ever."

"And?" Jay prompted.

A thin sheen of sweat broke out over Wilford's face. "You hate reporters with a white-hot passion."

"And?" Jay prompted.

"A-and if you ever laid eyes on me again, it would be me who was a missing person."

I held back a laugh.

"Very good. Now move."

Feeling bad for Wilford, I offered him a soft smile.

He returned it and chanced a glance up at Jay. "New girlfriend, Detective?"

"Oh no." I waved my hands in front of me, "I'm not his girlfriend. I'm just his—"

Jay circled my waist with his arm and jerked me to him. He splayed his other hand over my stomach and let out a possessive growl.

Wilford inclined his head and stepped aside for Jay and me to pass. He nodded at me. "Nice to meet the woman in his life. I was starting to think he was beyond hope, but with someone as pretty as you as his wife, he can't be all that bad."

His wife?

My jaw dropped open, but no sound came out.

Jay ushered me through the door. "She can talk me down from a lot of things, breaking you in two isn't one of them, Wilford. Go away. Now."

I stared wide-eyed at Jay as he led me down a long corridor that opened into a large room. I tried to stop, but Jay kept us moving.

"Wife?" I managed.

He ignored me as he led me through the station. Men and women were everywhere.

Some were at desks in cubicles. Others were coming out of what looked like a meeting room. Several were with people in cuffs.

Two men near a coffee machine spotted us and exchanged knowing looks before smiling. I was still stuck on the reporter assuming I was Jay's wife, and Jay not bothering to correct him.

A detective with medium-brown hair, wearing jeans and a casual shirt, lifted his cup of coffee. "Who's your *friend* there, Gonzales?"

Jay ignored him, steering me towards a glass door on the right. He pulled his keys out and unlocked it. The guy with the coffee headed our way. Jay opened the door for me and waited as I entered his office.

One look around and I wanted to leave. The man's office looked like a city dump. His house wasn't that way, which made me wonder how his office came to be in that state. "How can you find anything in here?"

He shrugged, tossing his keys on one of the many piles of folders on his desk. "I have a system."

"The 'hope rats come and file things for you' system?" I asked, staring around.

Jay snickered and sat in his chair behind the

desk. He slid his keyboard tray out and started typing.

"Mmm, since Gonzales is rude, I'd like to take a minute to introduce myself." The man with the coffee leaned on the doorframe. "I'm Romeo." He let his hazel gaze rake over me slowly.

Romeo? He couldn't be serious.

"Yeah, I just bet you are," I said with a snort.

He grinned. "Oh, a redhead with sass. Who'd have *thunk* it?"

"Go away, Rodriquez," Jay said, still typing. "If you don't, I'll let Gina beat the leaving hell out of you."

Romeo looked hopeful as he stepped closer to me. He wasn't bad on the eyes in any way, but I wasn't interested. He apparently didn't get the memo though, because he moved even closer, making skin-to-skin contact with me. "So, Gina, you're Gonzales's what?"

Annoyed, I let out a deep breath. "I'm the wife, if you ask that little reporter guy. As soon as Jay is done here, he's going to take me back home and pick up where he left off when he got called in."

Romeo smacked his lips a couple of times, obviously in need of water. "Which was where?"

I had to give him credit. Most people would have shut up and walked away. Not him. "Letting me play with his *tool* before he *nailed* me with his *hammer*."

I walked away from him and towards Jay, who had stopped typing and was staring at me with a slightly stunned yet amused expression on his face.

Jay licked his lower lip. "I'm hard already, baby."

"Why am I not shocked?" I shook my head and moved up next to him. I ran my hands over his shoulders.

He growled again, the sound deeper than before.

My gaze flicked to Romeo. Jay's growl didn't sound even close to human. I waited for Romeo to freak.

He lifted a brow, finding humor in Jay's response. "Gonna pull her onto your lap and make that official right here and now, or do you think you can hold it long enough to get her home?" asked Romeo.

I nibbled on Jay's ear. "Oh, he can hold it.

All. Night. Long."

Romeo watched us closely and tugged at the collar of his shirt. "Damn, I really need to start dating redheads. Got any sisters?"

I rubbed the back of Jay's neck lightly. "You work with him daily and don't kill him? I have a whole new level of respect for you."

"Thanks, baby, it's hard," Jay said, winking.

Romeo snickered and lifted his mug in the air, saluting me. "I like you. I normally loathe his women. And with the way he cycles through them, it's an endless line of abhorrence." As soon as he said it, he cringed. "I mean, I, uhh… shit. Um, well, he's never growled over the others before, if that helps. Crap. Going now."

He walked away.

The idea of Jay and his line of annoying women left me on edge. I yanked my hand off his neck as if his skin were toxic. In truth, it was. It made me do things I wouldn't normally do— like caress and cuddle.

That could be lethal, right?

Jay exhaled loudly and turned his monitor for me to see it better. "Scroll through and see if you recognize any of the names or descriptions."

I bent forward and avoided brushing against him as if he were carrying the plague.

He sighed. "Dammit, Gina, you're mad at me again. I can sense it."

"Why would I be mad?" I did my best to appear unaffected by Romeo's comments. I read the list of names on the screen, hoping my face was blank. The way Jay let out another long, exasperated breath, I don't think I quite pulled it off.

A young guy poked his head in. "Detective, the captain wants to see you."

Jay stood slowly, and for a second, I thought he might say something to me. He didn't. He did, however, avoid meeting my gaze on the way out.

None of the names stuck out to me, but I did manage to learn what areas of the city I didn't want to live in. The rec center was located smack-dab in the middle of one of them. I clicked through additional pages and stopped when I reached a password-protected file.

Curiosity got the best of me, and I tried just about everything I could think of for his password. Nothing worked.

Jay stopped in the doorway with Romeo close at his heels. "Fiery One," he said softly, his attention on me. "We need to go look into something for a case. You gonna be okay here for about an hour?"

Fiery One?

I nodded.

He gave me a slight nod before heading out.

I keyed in the nickname he seemed to like to call me and much to my surprise, the file opened.

The shock didn't end there. No. I sat there, staring at photos of myself at various stages of life—each one depicting any slayer-related cases the police had ended up involved in. I always carried fake identification on the off chance human authorities happened upon me beating the living hell out of a supernatural. It's not as if I could use the "he was a bloodsucker" excuse and not land in the funny farm or a state penitentiary.

Jay's file on me had every account of me ever getting hurt that I could think of, plus a few I'd forgotten about. Several of the cases had left me battered to the point I'd been transported to the private medical facility that catered to supernaturals. The suspect in each incident had been listed as "unknown." A notation added at a later date had "deceased" marked behind "unknown."

I knew what that meant. Someone had followed my trail, taking out whoever had harmed me.

Sitting there, I became increasingly aware of what Jay had done for me. I swallowed hard before closing out of that file and covering any trace of me having been there.

I went back to looking through recent entries, hoping to find any hint of what might have happened to any of my fellow slayers.

The minutes turned into an hour without anything catching my attention and no sign of Jay. My stomach grew tight, and I began to pace his office. There was something happening to supernaturals in the city. I didn't know what but I knew it was leading to more deaths. If Jay was hurt, I wasn't sure what I'd do.

Nerves had gotten the better of me, and without thought, I began straightening his office, cleaning it, too worried to sit down.

As time moved onward, I was positive Jay was lying dead in an alley. Every horrible scenario possible had played through my mind at least twice. As I threw away the last of what was obviously trash, I felt the heavy weight of someone's stare on my back.

I turned to find Jay in the doorway, watching me with a smirk on his handsome face.

The normal me would have yelled at him or kicked his ass or all of the above. The new me, the one who was struggling with strange feelings for him, burst into tears.

He came at me fast. "Gina, what's wrong? Did you figure out which slayers…?"

I slipped my arms around his waist and put my cheek to his chest, crying even harder.

Stroking my hair, he tried to calm me. "Talk to me, baby."

"I thought something happened to you," I whispered, knowing he could hear me because of his lycan abilities. I fisted his T-shirt and kissed his chest gently. "I can't decide if I want to kiss you or kill you."

He tugged the back of my long hair, forcing me to look up at him. Confusion shone in his chocolate gaze, along with something else. Something I couldn't quite read. The edge of his mouth drew upwards. "If I get a say, can I go with option number one?"

I laughed through my tears and then swatted his rock-hard abs. "Dammit, Jay, was it too much to call my cell and tell me you were all right but running late? You know something big went down tonight, that slayers were lost. You had to understand I'd be here thinking the worst when you didn't show. We swore we'd text each other updates about things. No text is on my phone, Jayson."

I kept going, reading him the riot act. He, in turn, put his hands on my shoulders, rubbing them softly, appearing slightly pleased by my antics.

"This is not funny. I was worried about you."

"I know, baby. I'm sorry." Nodding, he glanced around his newly cleaned office. "Can I ask you something?"

I glared at him.

He grinned. "As my wife, when I come home late in the future, are you going to channel your aggression into scrubbing the finish out of our tub or are you going to kick my ass?"

I blinked, and then caught the joke. "Jackass."

Waggling his brows, he dipped his head and kissed the tip of my nose. "Yep, but since I'm a jackass who is back in one piece, does that at least win me some brownie points with you?"

I put my palm to his scruffy cheek and ran my thumb over his smooth, full lips. Our gazes locked and sexual tension thickened the air. "Yes."

"Holy shit, Gonzales," Romeo said, entering the office and killing the mood. "Your girlfriend managed to find a desk under all the clutter. Oh, and a floor. Oh, and a—"

I smiled as Jay pulled back, standing tall.

He took my hand in his and faced his friend. "Yeah, trust me when I say her aggression could have been channeled in a lot less constructive ways."

"You hate people touching anything in here," Romeo countered. "Guess you just hate it when people who aren't her do it, huh?"

Jay surprised me by lifting our joined hands and kissing the back of mine. "You ready to go?"

"He's hooked," Romeo said. "He's flat-out

avoiding my questions and not losing his mind about his office being, dare I say, clean."

I smiled at Romeo. "Believe it or not, I think the man really does have a system. I simply gathered it all up and filed it accordingly. I'm thinking he'll be bitching at me for years to come about it all though."

He stared at our joined hands. "Doubtful. On any *other* note than this, because Jay will kick my ass, what do you say we grab a bite to eat? It's getting late, and Jay here tells me you're a night owl for the most part too. Plus, he swears you love to eat. Up for it, or are you two going to head back to his place and pick up where you left off?"

It took me a second to catch on. I squeezed Jay's hand and teared up again. "Um, I am hungry again."

He pulled me into another hug. "Let's get something to eat, baby."

When I realized what he was doing, I drew back and socked him in the arm. "Sure."

He smiled wide.

Jerk.

11

I LAUGHED AS ROMEO LAUNCHED INTO ANOTHER story of something he and Jay had gone through during their first few years on the force. I knew they were trying to keep my mind off what was happening in the slayer community and I appreciated it.

I'd already spent the first half of our time at the supernatural-friendly diner in awe that Romeo was like Jay—a shifter. He'd spent equally as long shocked by the news I was a slayer. He took the news well. Not everyone did. There was still just enough tension between slayers and supernaturals that one didn't always have to look too far to find hostility.

I took a sip of iced tea and nearly choked on it when Romeo finished his story.

Jay patted my back, his body brushing close to mine in the booth. "It wasn't that funny."

I rubbed my upper chest to chase away the burning sensation. "It's fucking hilarious. I wish I could have seen you sitting in a baby pool, pissed because a garden hose was in the way while you were chasing a suspect."

He nipped at me with a smile on his face. I took the other half of the monster-sized burger they'd served me and stuck it in his mouth. He laughed, and I stole a carrot stick from his plate as he worked on the rest of my burger.

Romeo watched our actions and shook his head. "I know you cleared up the whole not-really-a-couple thing, but are you sure you're not shitting me? I may not be an expert on relationships, but the two of you seem pretty damn comfy with one another."

"Why wouldn't I be comfortable with Jay?" I asked, sipping my drink again.

"I have friends who are girls, erm, women, and I can't think of any time we finished each other's sentences and ate off each other's plates. Hell, I can't think of a time any girlfriend I've ever had did that with me either."

I tipped my head. "Ever think it's you?"

Jay laughed.

Romeo blushed. "I think I like her. A lot."

"You would," Jay said.

A tiny bit of mustard stuck to the side of his stubble-covered chin. I lifted a napkin and eyed the spot, as I did whenever it happened to him. He took it from me and wiped, lifting his head more. I nodded, indicating he got it, and we went back to eating.

Romeo snorted. "Yeah, I'm not buying the not-a-couple bit. Christ, you act like you've been a couple for a hell of a long time. You cleaned his office, and he ordered food for you without him even having to ask what you like."

I looked at Jay. "If I kill your friend, will you miss him?"

"Nope," he said, chuckling.

As Harley, one of the diner's owners, approached our table, I couldn't help but notice his shirt. It was shiny and straight out of the '70s, with its pale purple color and a print of tiny dancing men on it, striking a disco pose. Harley wasn't much older than me, but he dressed as if he was hoping "Stayin' Alive" would break the top ten.

As if on cue, the Bee Gees began to play

from the jukebox. I crawled over Jay and Harley put his hand out to me. I took it and couldn't contain my laughter as we instantly launched into the hustle.

Harley rolled with laughter as well, to the point he nearly cried.

Charles, his soon-to-be husband, came from the back-office area and shook his head. "I knew Gina was here if you were playing this song."

"Join in," I said to Charles.

His eyes widened. "Pass."

My attention went to Jay.

He shook his head. "No."

"You suck," I said, bumping hips with Harley.

The other patrons watched us, smiling. Some took pictures, and I'm sure video. I didn't care. Harley was tons of fun and someone I considered a friend. So was Charles.

The song drew to an end, and Harley hugged me. "You're putting too long between coming in here."

"I know. I'm not at the rec center like I used to be," I returned before turning and climbing over Jay.

My foot caught on his, and I landed in his lap.

His hands went to my hips, and his body stiffened. He grunted.

I looked over my shoulder at him as I sat, my back to his front. "Why hello there, sailor."

Harley snorted and put his hand on Jay's shoulder. "You two do the dirty yet?"

Jay glanced at me like the idea had a lot of merit.

"Uh, no," I supplied.

Harley waggled his brows. "Keep sitting on his lap like that and you will."

That motivated me to move back to my spot in the booth, between Jay and the window.

Charles chuckled as he brought us drink refills. "All kidding aside, is there a reason you two haven't started to date yet? We have a pool going. I think Myra is going to win."

I glanced at Jay and raised a brow. "I'm almost afraid to ask what the pool is and what she picked."

Harley beamed and ran a hand through his brown hair. "It started as when the two of you would finally have sex. Myra made us change that to start dating. She said the other board was tacky. And she also said a quarter to never, since you're both commitment-phobic."

Romeo tapped the table. "What's the buy-in?"

"A buck," said Charles.

Romeo tossed a dollar on the table. "I pick this week."

"Oh, is there an inside scoop we should know about?" questioned Harley.

"Romeo," said Jay sternly.

"What?" Romeo winked. "I'm staying with this week."

"Want me to climb under the table and blow him?" I asked as Jay put his large hand on my thigh, engulfing it.

"You'd win, Romeo," said Jay.

Charles, Harley, and Romeo laughed.

"Is it me or does Jay look hopeful?" asked Harley. "We might want to change our pick to this month too."

Charles rolled his eyes and put his hands on Harley's shoulders. "Okay, we'll let you be. Nice to meet you, Romeo."

Romeo nodded as they walked off.

I touched Jay's hand. "We should totally go

back to my place and do it. That would teach Myra not to bet against us."

"Okay," said Jay, making a move to stand.

I grabbed his hand. "No. Kidding."

He flashed a sexy smile. "I know, but that doesn't mean the idea was shit."

My attention went to Romeo.

He licked his lips. "Tell me about yourself, Gina. I know all about Jay, and now you've heard all about me. What about you? You from the area?"

"Yes and no," I replied, sliding closer to Jay in the booth. "I moved here when I was younger."

"And before that?"

"I didn't live here," I said evenly. I wasn't big into discussing my past.

"Oh, I see why the two of you get along," he replied, putting more ketchup on his plate. "Both of you just love sharing."

I smiled, taking pity on him. "I really don't know where I'm from originally. I wasn't old enough to remember where I lived. I can tell you that I moved around a lot when I was younger because of my father's job."

"Army brat?"

"No. Daughter of an FBI agent, and then a foster kid for a bit before being adopted," I replied.

Jay stiffened. That wasn't something I shared with too many people. "Your biological father is in the FBI?"

"I don't know if he still is. I just know that he was," I said, thinking back to what I could vividly remember about him. "He had vests, shirts, and jackets that had FBI printed across them. I remember a gun safe that was locked down like Fort Knox. He'd come home and go there first, taking off his weapon and badge, putting them both in the safe. And I remember him hugging me and telling me he had to go hunt bad men, and he'd be back in a few days. After my mother died, he took me with him for a bit."

"I can look into him," said Jay as he put an arm around me in the booth. "Got a name for me to go from?"

"Daddy," I said, in all seriousness. "He seemed really tall to me when I was little. He might actually be, or my kid perspective warped that. I remember he had short black hair. Green eyes like me, because my mother would point out that while I got her hair, I got his eyes and his temper. He used to sing to me before bed. Sometimes he'd play guitar too. And I remember him kneeling before me, his hands on my shoulders as he cried. He told me he was sorry that he had to go, but I wouldn't be safe with him. And he needed to know I was safe. Then he walked out of my life."

"How old were you when this happened?" asked Jay.

"Four."

Romeo watched me closely, narrowing his gaze. I'd seen Jay do something similar and guessed he was reading my body language like a good detective would. "You remember more about him than that, but you're not sure if your mind is playing tricks on you. As if you've seen so much that maybe your mind has filled in the blanks with wrong information."

I had to force the French fry down, my mouth was suddenly that dry.

"He was the first man to break your heart. He told you he'd never let anything happen to you and that'd he'd never leave you. But he left anyways," Romeo said.

Jay tapped the table. "Stop."

Romeo nodded. "Sorry. Sometimes the reading-someone thing just happens."

"I take it you've got a little something more than lycan in your mix there, huh?" I asked, though the answer was obvious.

"Yeah. A little bit," replied Romeo.

Romeo continued to eye me as he sat across from us in the diner. I knew he was still reading me. I also more than knew he probably couldn't stop, even if he wanted to.

"Say it." I stared at him, my temper even. I wasn't upset with him. My past was something I didn't enjoy discussing, but I knew Romeo wasn't digging to be cruel or to pick at old scabs. "I see the wheels in your head spinning. You'll only tell Jay later when I'm not around."

Jay caressed my inner thigh, making my body heat.

Romeo shifted awkwardly in the booth. "Something horrific happened when you were little, and people assume you were too young at age three to fully remember it. They're wrong. Until your teens, you thought it was a dream, a nightmare, but you remember enough that it still haunts you. When you came into your slayer gifts and learned what was really out there, you realized it might not be a dream after all. That what you remembered happening, could very well have actually happened. Trusting Jay was a major step for you. Even more so than trusting your friend's father who's a vampire."

I simply listened to him. He wasn't telling me anything I didn't already know. Oddly, I felt removed from the emotions of it all. As if at some point over the span of my life, I'd developed a coping mechanism, and it was avoiding my emotions in connection to events of the past.

I eyed Romeo. "Are you planning to tell him the rest, or would you rather I excuse myself and go stand in the restroom, so you can say it without worrying if I'll break down and cry?"

He sipped his soda, looking as if he were in a trance of sorts as he stared glassy-eyed at me. "You were so scared when you woke up, and everything in your life turned upside down. You didn't understand what a slayer was, let alone what was happening to you. Your friend helped you. She told you the truth of what was out there, and the entire time she told you, your chest was tight—not because there's more to the world than humans know about, but because it meant your memories of your childhood may not have been invented. And if they were real, that meant your mother's death wasn't quick or natural. So much so that you didn't share your memories with anyone—not even your best friends."

He was right. It had been a confusing time in my life. One I didn't care to go back and repeat again. I still wasn't sure if my calling was a blessing or a curse. It was all I had so I went with it.

Romeo spoke again. "You went on instinct to start with as a slayer. You hadn't met another one or been trained at all. You killed whatever you came across—aside from your friend and her family. And that haunts you. Were they all bad? Did you mistake any of their intentions? Would you have killed Jay when you'd first met him, had you known he was a shifter? Would you have ended him without even getting to know him?

"You don't trust easily and let very few people in. To date, you've let two men under your armor as an adult. The first broke your heart as well—walking out without any real warning, just like your father had. And just like with your father, you made no attempt to stop him or to search for him later. You simply shut down your emotions and carried on with life."

My thoughts went to Samuel, and how much it had stung when he'd decided he wanted more than I could offer. He'd done as Romeo had said and simply announced he was leaving and that he was done. That was that. I'd not seen or heard from him again. It didn't haunt me. I didn't actually think about it at all. I understood it was because I didn't want to feel the hurt of it all again.

"Jay is the only other man you've let in to that point," said Romeo, his gaze fixated on the table. "But you aren't even sure how that happened. You just know that it didn't take you long to accept him into your daily life, which surprised you. And since meeting him, you can't stop running your earlier kills through your head. You have guilt because you think you could have hurt him without knowing him— maybe even killed him while on slayer automatic pilot. You sit up at night, running the years

before you met him through your head,
wondering how many innocent supernatural
lives you've taken."

I ate another fry even though my stomach
was starting to protest.

"None," said Romeo.

I stopped chewing.

"You didn't take any innocent lives, Gina,"
he said slowly. "Part of our line of lycans is the
ability to sense or smell death on others. Not in
the way you think. Someone who's taken the
lives of the innocent has a certain feeling or
scent about them. You lack it. If you'd have told
Jay about your concerns, he could have told you
the same thing and saved you all these years of
worrying." He offered a soft smile. "As much as
you'll deny this, you're a good person. You have
a pure heart. A heart you pretend not to have,
but it's there…broken and battered, but there."

I eyed my butter knife, considering using it.

He snickered.

Jay nudged me, and I put my head against
his shoulder.

"You can stab him if you want. If you don't,
I'll do it later because he brought this up,"
said Jay.

I kissed his shoulder and paused, wondering why I kept doing random acts like that with him. "Nah, I kind of like him. And what he can do doesn't freak me out. It's familiar. Kind of. But that part of my life is closed now.

Romeo leaned back in the booth. "That's not really true, Gina. The fact you never once killed an innocent supernatural says you didn't close it all the way off, even though it was your end goal."

That made me tense. "I can't do it very well anymore."

"What?" Jay asked. "*You?* You can read others like Romeo?"

"No," Romeo and I answered in unison.

"It's not the same," he said. "I feel it and just sort of know. Gina used to *see* it and feel it. When she closed her eyes at night, things would just come to her, and during the day, knowledge she shouldn't have would niggle at the back of her mind. It still does from time to time, especially when she's in life-or-death situations. It's when she tends to shut off and let that sixth sense help guide her."

"Slayers don't possess anything above added

strength, agility, healing, and immortality," Jay said.

Romeo grinned. "Guess she has a little bit more than just slayer in her mix, huh?"

A slow smile slid across my face. "Yep."

12

"WERE YOUR BIRTH PARENTS SUPERNATURAL?" asked Jay, his head resting on mine as I continued to lean against his shoulder.

I nodded. "Yes. I have very few memories of my mom. My hair is the same color as hers. That much I know. When I try to think about her, I just feel this overwhelming sense of love. And then I remember...I remember details about her death, but some of it is fuzzy. I do remember my father telling me that she was fierce, and he knew I could be too. It was in my blood."

"Was she a slayer?" Jay rubbed my knee.

"Honestly, I don't know."

Romeo watched me. "Tell Jay what you remember about your father."

I shot him a hard look and then let out a long breath. "That he was more than human."

Romeo lifted a brow. "That's it? Really? I know what you know. Try another one."

I threw a fry at him.

He laughed.

Taking a deep breath, I pressed closer to Jay before speaking. "He was always surrounded by a lot of men. They were almost always at the house. Some lived with us full time. The rest came over a lot. Some all at once while he'd stand on a raised area of a big room to talk with them. Two of the men were always with me when my father had to leave for work. I didn't understand why they were always around but there was no reason to question. It was how it had always been. Looking back, I understand now."

Romeo nodded. "They were there to protect you. You remember them being kind to you, playing with you, always being there for you, and you loved them like they were uncles."

"Yes, but their faces, like my parents, are so hard to remember now that I'm older. I just remember the feel of them—that I was totally safe with them. And I remember…" I glanced at Romeo.

He nodded. "That they could change into wolves, like your father."

Jay gasped. "Wait. Your father is a wolf shifter? No. I'd smell that on you."

Romeo caught my attention and motioned to Jay. "Tell him what you remember even if you're not sure the memory is real."

A shaky laugh escaped me. "I'm not sure any of it is real. So, you'll have to be more specific."

"The time you were swinging in the back-yard and something bad happened," prompted Romeo.

I thought about what he meant and then nodded. "We were somewhere else. Not home. I remember that I couldn't stay home with my mom, but I don't remember why. My dad and his men were hunting something. I don't know what. They never let me know any details. We were all staying in a big house that wasn't our home, and we didn't stay in it long, but it had a swing set that I really liked out back," I said softly.

"I was allowed out back alone, and they

were all just inside. They could see me, and I could see them. I remember waving at my father as he spoke to the men with him, and him stopping to wave back. Then when he went back to talking, a huge wolf came over the fence and landed in the backyard with me. I wasn't afraid of him. Why would I be? Everyone I'd ever known until then had been kind and caring."

Jay tightened his hold on my leg slightly.

"I was excited. The men and my dad were my only playmates then, so his men would often shift and play-chase me. I'd pretend to chase them too, and they humored me. In my mind, the newcomer was there to play. I ran to the wolf because I wasn't very good at telling them apart then. There were just too many around all the time. This one looked at me differently though. Not like the ones I'd grown up with. And when I tried to pet him, he snapped at my hand. I tried to kiss him to make him less angry, and he knocked me to the ground and opened his mouth wide, putting it over my throat and pinning me there. I still thought it was a fun game, so I was giggling, having the time of my life."

"Christ, I'm going to throw up," said Jay, looking pale.

I lifted a brow and glanced at Romeo. "Spoiler alert. I lived. Should we ruin the story for him and tell him as much?"

Romeo grinned and winked. "How is it you were fine, Gina? What happened? How is it your father could get you safely away from a shifter who had his jaws around your tiny throat?"

I took a deep breath. "I heard my father yelling for the wolf to release me at once. He warned it, telling it what he'd do if it didn't. That only made the wolf growl more and he actually started to pull me by my neck in the grass in the direction of the fence. Again, I thought it was the best game ever, and I couldn't understand why my dad sounded so angry. He'd never yelled at anyone for playing with me before."

I sat up and stared at my plate of food, the events of the past rushing over me. "Then all of a sudden the sky got dark, and there was a huge boom of thunder that scared me enough to make me cry. I couldn't see my father very well from where I was. When I tried to turn my head to see him the wolf's teeth pressed harder on my neck. It hurt, so I just lay there, scared of the pending storm, but not of the wolf who was going to tear my throat out.

"Then it sounded like there were thousands of wolves around me. I get it wasn't that many, but I was little, so it felt like a ton. And my concept of pack was skewed. It was never called pack around me. It was called family. I fully understood that my family was there, around me. Deep down I knew it wasn't a game anymore. That something was wrong, and they were all scared and mad. They wanted to hurt the wolf with me, but I still didn't understand why still. They never hurt each other. They'd get upset with each other sometimes, and I'd tell them it's not nice to hit, but they never felt like they felt that day—like they wanted to do far more than hit the wolf with me."

"They wanted to rip the fucking asshole's head off," said Jay, as if he more than understood what was going through their minds, even without being there.

A soft laugh came from me. "I get that as an adult. But then it was so different for me."

Romeo grinned. "Your father and the

others like him never exposed you to the violent side of it all. They treated you like a princess, and they all wanted you safe and far from harm. It makes sense. Children are precious gifts in our world. And daughters are rare— very rare. The pack we're in is huge, and to date, no females have been born to the mated pairs. And only a small percentage of the pairs have had a child. One pair has two boys, a set of twins. We're all extremely protective of the young. And should one of us be blessed with a daughter I'd feel bad for her. She'd have hundreds of uncles standing between her and dating."

I couldn't help but laugh. "Oh, I'm sure of it. Jay isn't the best to deal with when I'm dating. I'd feel horrible for a girl in your pack. Poor thing would be put in an ivory tower, never to be exposed to the evil ways of men."

Romeo glanced at Jay and then focused on me. "Gina, Jay isn't like that with every woman he's around. You're a special case."

"No, I'm not. He was like this with Lindsay. I'd say more so with her, even," I said, telling the truth. Jay was very protective of Lindsay. He always had been.

Jay's entire body tensed as he sat next to me. "Not true."

Romeo cleared his throat. "You never told Jay how your father managed to safely get you away from the wolf."

I thought back to it all again. "The sky kept getting darker and darker, and there was lightning with more thunder. I was scared of thunderstorms then, so it freaked me out big time. And it felt like it came out of nowhere. One second the weather had been beautiful out and then, bam, it was dark as night. My uncles, or my father's men, were shouting at him to stop before he lost full control and ended up hurting me. They kept yelling for him to pull back on his power. I moved my head more, ignoring the pain of the wolf's teeth and looked at my dad. His eyes were super green—glowing almost. And the storm worsened.

"The wolf didn't let me go. He yanked me again, and this time his teeth pierced my skin. I cried because it hurt, and my dad roared, broke the other men's hold on him, and ran at me. I remember him jumping high into the air, one arm changing with fur on it and the other normal. He pointed the normal one at the wolf who had me, and it cried out, clearly hurt. It released my throat, and I tried to help it. My father shouted 'no' at me and then I was suddenly up and off the ground, going backwards, but no one was holding me. No one was there. One of my uncles jumped up and caught me and cradled me against him before rushing into the house with me. I didn't see what else happened but later that night, my father was holding me, and he apologized for scaring me with the storm. He also said that he'd set fire to the world to keep me safe."

Romeo nodded slightly. "Your father was a shifter who also possessed magik. It's not unheard of, but it's not something you run into all the time. And none of us really talk about it outside of our packs."

I'd never realized it was a thing until recently. I'd honestly thought I'd imagined it all because even when I'd come into my slayer gifts, I'd never been exposed to a shifter who could wield magik. "Meeting Exavier, my friend Lindsay's husband, helped me to understand that what I remembered about my dad might not be wrong. It wasn't until I met Exavier that I knew it was even possible to be both a shifter and a magik. He's both. But he feels different than my dad used to feel. Like Exavier is more magik than a wolf. But my dad was more wolf than magik."

"If that's the case, it makes sense why his own men would try to stop him from using magik," said Romeo. "They were probably afraid of his control over it. Afraid you'd be hurt by him without him meaning to."

I took a drink and then bit my lower lip. "After that happened, my father made me sit and learn what every man who was always around us looked like in wolf form. And he kept telling me over and over again that not all wolves are good. He was very clear that I wasn't allowed to run up and hug another wolf again unless I knew him. He was upset that I couldn't smell differences. That I couldn't do what he could."

Romeo winked. "See? There is more to you than just slayer."

I shook my head. "No. I'm just a slayer."

Jay rubbed my thigh and leaned close, kissing the side of my head.

"Gina," Romeo said, his voice low. "You

know the day will come when you'll have to face him again."

He meant my father, and I knew it. Shaking my head, I kept my gaze averted from him. "No. It won't."

"You sound sure of yourself. Why?"

I ran my finger over the glass of the window. "Because he blames me for my mother's death. Before he finally left me at some random hospital, he could barely even look at me anymore. He tried the single-parent gig for a bit, but he was done. I was put into the system straight away, and it was almost two years before I somehow ended up placed with a couple who later adopted me. It's been over twenty years since I saw my father, standing there, unable to look at me before he walked away. As you can see, he's not here."

Jay pulled me against his large body.

"Have you ever stopped to think maybe it's not you he blames, but rather himself?" Romeo asked.

Jay hit the table. "No more."

I snuggled against him. "It's okay. Really."

"No, baby," he said. "It's not. I feel you hurting on the inside."

I gave him a questioning look, but he didn't elaborate.

"Gina, you blame yourself for her death, don't you?" Romeo asked, ignoring Jay's protest and warning. "*He'd* have found her anyway. He could smell her fear and hear her heart pounding."

My hand found Jay's and I laced my fingers through his as Romeo continued to talk about my past.

"Your tiny gasp didn't alert him to where the two of you were hiding. He already knew, but he was toying with you both. You can stop blaming yourself. It wasn't your fault, and I don't think your father blames you either."

I looked up, a sense of peace starting to settle over me. It didn't take away from the guilt I still carried over living when she didn't. "I still don't understand why he'd hurt us. Why he'd kill her and try to kill me. He was my father's best friend. His second-in-command, and all he'd ever been to me was kind and loving. I trusted him so much. Then I woke up from a nap, terrified for my mother. I ran to her and told her what I saw. She didn't question me. She ran through the house with me as fast as she could because she was far into her second pregnancy."

I took an unnatural interest in the artificial sweeteners on the table as I continued. "She cried out like she was in pain and fell, dropping me. She was clutching her stomach and telling me to run. To run and do what felt natural. To hide like she knew I could. But she didn't get up at first, and I didn't want to go without her. Looking back, I think she might have gone into labor.

"She pushed up, took my hand and only managed to get me to a closet. I wouldn't let go of her hand and made her come in too. She held me against her and told me over and over how sorry she was that she wasn't going to be able to stop him. And she told me that he wasn't my uncle anymore—that something bad had ahold of him and not to be afraid and not to look."

Jay kissed my temple.

I glanced out of the window of the diner and noticed the same man I'd seen outside of the vampire club, standing at the end of the street. He was watching the diner, his hair pulled up, wearing faded jeans and a black T-shirt.

Thoughts of my father flooded back to me as I stared at the stranger. "My father came in, and he started to shout. Other men were with him, and they all tackled the one who'd hurt my mom. I was so scared that I refused to come out of the closet. My father had to crawl over my mother's dead body to get me and lift me out. He was crying. I was crying. And I remember him holding me so tight that the two men who guarded me had to pry me out of his arms. They told him that he'd break me without meaning to."

Closing my eyes, I tried to wash the memories from my mind again. To bury them in the secret vault that I keep deep within me. The one that I almost never opened to avoid the pain.

When I opened my eyes, the man under the streetlamp was gone.

Jay clutched my thigh so tightly, I hissed. He stopped and rubbed it gently. "Gina, why didn't you tell me any of this?"

I couldn't help but smile as I looked at him. "Because I hoped to one day be here, in a diner, eating a burger while your buddy—the oracle, who can shed with the best of them—filled you in."

Romeo laughed.

Jay didn't.

I hated seeing him worry about me. I twisted more, leaned up and pressed a kiss to his cheek. "I spent nearly all my life thinking my memories of it were all wrong. Even when I learned the truth about supernaturals, I still thought I was wrong. I didn't know shifters could possess magik. Six months ago, I learned they can. None of this changes anything. It is what it is."

"I can sense you're upset," he whispered, his lips skimming my jawline.

My entire body lit with need. I smiled against his skin. "Can you sense what I'm feeling now?"

I meant it to be a joke to lighten the mood.

When Jay growled, sounding possessive, and jerked me against him, I gulped. "G-guess so."

Romeo tossed his head back and laughed.

I blushed. "I didn't know Jay could read people too."

"He can't. He can read *you*. Not others."

I stilled. "Why me?"

Jay glanced at Romeo, and when Romeo

nodded, Jay squeezed my leg to the point of pain again. I grabbed his fingers and pried them off me one by one. "Ouch."

"Shit," he said, reaching to rub me again. "I'm sorry, baby. I didn't mean to hurt you."

Catching his hand in mid-motion, I put it on his own leg and patted it gently. "No problem. But avoid touching me for a little bit. I'm thinking next time something gets you worked up, you'll accidentally tear my leg clean off."

He made a move to come at me, and I shoved a fry into his mouth, making him laugh.

Romeo smiled.

My gaze went to the window, and I couldn't help but think about the fallen slayers. I was laughing and talking about the past when my fellow slayers were under attack.

I checked my phone again to be sure I didn't miss a text update from Zachariah.

I didn't.

Jay touched my cheek. "Hey, we'll hear something soon."

"The downed slayers you were telling me about?" asked Romeo as he looked at Jay.

Jay nodded.

"I should be out there patrolling the streets," I said. "Not sitting here."

"Baby," he said, his hand still on my cheek, "if Zachariah wanted you out there, he'd have called you in, right?"

"Yes." Didn't mean it felt right.

His arm moved around me, and he dragged me into his powerful frame. "You're good where you are. If he calls, we'll all go to help, okay?"

Smiling, I stayed with him, enjoying being held. I didn't want to overthink what was happening between us. I just knew I needed the comfort he was providing.

13

My cell rang, but it was the ringtone for Lindsay, so I didn't panic, but answered quickly. "Are you okay? Is the baby all right?"

"Gina, are you okay?" she asked, sounding breathless.

I sighed. Lindsay had probably heard slayers had fallen and thought one was me. I never gave any thought to texting her that I was okay and safe. "I'm fine, hon. Promise. You know if I go down, Zachariah will call you. You're my emergency contact."

"I thought you changed that to Jay," she said.

"I started to change it all over to Jay, but that seemed weird. Like Jay would want to be in charge of end-of-life decisions for me."

Jay growled. "Anyone hurts you, and I'll tear their fucking arms off and beat them to death with them."

Lindsay laughed softly. "Kind of late to be with him, isn't it? I didn't interrupt some hot monkey sex, did I?"

"Hot monkey sex with Jay?" I asked. "Wait, you're serious?"

Jay stiffened.

Lindsay grew quiet. "Gina, Jay and I haven't been a couple in a long time, and I'm married now and six months pregnant with my husband's child. Jay and I didn't have a relationship. We had an understanding."

I held the phone tighter. "I know you're mated and not seeing Jay anymore. Why are you stressing this? Also, have the two of you been talking and comparing notes? He gave me the same speech about fuck buddies not in love."

"It's important you don't see Jay painted with the brush of being my ex," she returned softly. "Also, you need to understand that Jay first came into my life because he wanted to know about *you*. He'd seen us together. He was interested in *you*. Not me. You didn't pay him any attention. That was long ago."

Confused, I tipped my head, my hand finding Jay's thigh. "Why the hell are we talking about him like he's a painting metaphor? And what do you mean, he first came into your life asking about *me*?"

"Gina," she scolded.

I rolled my eyes. The woman was horrible at mothering me. "What, *Mom*?"

"Can you try for two seconds to be less you and listen?" she asked.

I grunted. "Fine. I'll try."

"Please don't see Jay as my ex," she stressed. "He's so much more than that. Look at him and see him for who and what he is. Gina, stop fighting nature. Give in."

"Listen, Linds, I get you want us all to play nicely together. I respect that. Jay and I are friends. Good friends. You don't have to worry about that falling apart now that you're doing the mom-and-wife gig." I kept my hand on Jay's leg, not really paying much mind to it. "But, let's be honest here. He may be hot, but hot only gets you so far if you have issues with commitment and see women as something to tally up."

Lindsay's laughter was loud. "True enough. He did have issues in the past with being loyal to his bed partners but, Gina, he had a good reason. And trust me, hon, that's in his past."

I arched a brow. "How, exactly, is there a good reason to screw your way through tons of women?"

Jay grunted.

I glanced up and held the phone out to him. "Here. Talk to your ex-hookup buddy. She is trying very hard to get me to paint you with a brush or something. Also, I think, but I can't be sure, that she's trying to make you out to be a saint for bagging a ton of chicks."

Jay took the phone. "Lindsay?"

I couldn't hear her side of the conversation, but from Jay's expression, it was a doozy. He was quiet for a bit before he spoke. "You heard her."

I glanced at Romeo who appeared surprised.

"You don't know, do you?" Romeo questioned.

"Know what?" I asked.

"How he feels about you and who you are to him," Romeo said as Jay began to argue with Lindsay, though I wasn't sure about what.

I glanced at Jay and then back to Romeo. "What do you mean, how he feels about me?

I'm a friend he met via his ex-hook-up buddy, or if you ask her, she met him because he asked about me. Right. And sure, the last six months have been different for us, but Jay and I don't see each other as more than really good friends."

As I said it, I knew I felt more than that for him, but didn't want to say it out loud.

Romeo closed his eyes a second and then stared at me, a huge smile spreading across his face. "The guy has women throwing themselves at him all the time. But not you. You don't toss yourself at him. You make him work for every bit of affection you offer him."

My brows met. "Should I be a Jay groupie? I like to think I have more respect for myself than that."

Truth was, I was totally turning into a Jay groupie. I wasn't sure what was worse, having a crazy master vampire who wanted to use darkness to either kill me or shag me, or realizing I wasn't just falling for Jay—I'd already fallen for him.

My eyes widened. "Shit."

Romeo snorted before taking another drink of his soda. "Perfect. This is perfect."

"Put him on the phone," Jay demanded loudly, pulling my attention to him as he gripped my phone to the point I thought he might shatter it. There was a pregnant pause. "Tell me exactly why you had Lindsay call, because we both know *you* already knew Gina wasn't one of the downed slayers." He listened for another moment, and his face paled. "Are you sure?"

"Jay?" I asked.

He ignored me as he spoke to Exavier, Lindsay's mate.

I snapped my fingers in Jay's face, unconcerned with how rude I was being. "Jayson?"

He paled even more, his gaze moving to me as he continued to speak to Exavier. "She's with me and fine right now. I'm not going to let her out of my sight. Yes, I'll make her spend the night with me."

"What?" I asked, sitting up straight and making a grab for my phone.

Jay held it out of reach and pinned me to the back of the booth with one arm as he kept talking. "No. I won't. Call my cell if you hear anything else. She'll be with me. Don't come here right now with everything that's going on. I don't want to deal with a rock star Prince of Darkness who accidentally gets a darkness whammy on arrival. Yeah, I'll keep you posted. Do the same."

He hung up and handed me my phone. I snatched it away from him and pushed on his arm, trying to get free. He released me from my pinned-in position.

"You," he said sternly, "are coming home with me and spending the night. Maybe more than one night. Get used to it, and there is no point arguing. I'll hogtie your stubborn, sexy ass."

I cast him a suspicious look as a huge smile spread across my face. "Is this a ploy to get to use your tool to hammer me?"

Jay growled. "Dammit, this isn't funny. I was just told the two slayers who were missing are now thought dead. There was apparently a shit-ton of blood in each of their houses that match their blood types. No bodies have been found yet, but Zachariah and Exavier think they're dead."

I stopped smiling. I tried to stand to go to Zachariah's and check in personally.

Jay grabbed me. "No."

"Jay—"

"Gina, something is going down. Something big," he said softly. "Exavier told me in no uncertain terms that you are in serious danger—that something massive is happening, and his hands are tied with something where he is or he'd be here to help."

He opened my cell, removed the battery and something else, before he really *did* pick it up and squeeze until it broke. My eyes widened.

He looked at me, moisture coating his brown eyes. "Until we figure out what's going on, you're not reporting in. Got it?"

"Jay—"

His jaw set. "Got it?"

"What right do you have to bark orders at me?"

Licking his lips, he locked gazes with me. "Baby, you have no idea just how much say I have when it comes to you."

I groaned.

"Tell me you understand and agree to stay near me until this is fixed."

I opened my mouth to argue.

"Gina, tell me!"

The force in which he asked made me sit back a little. Stunned, I nodded.

He dropped the broken pieces of my phone on the table and pushed them away. "I need you to respect my wishes on this. I need you to stop being stubborn and to do as I say."

"Tell her the truth," said Romeo.

Jay snarled. "Shut up."

"Tell me what truth?" I asked, looking at the men.

Neither said a word.

Male bonding sucked.

I was about to comment when I looked at my phone. "Jay, if I'm in danger, that means I could lead it back to you. I can't go to your house."

Romeo laughed. "Showing up at an alpha's house is like declaring war on the pack. There are only so many slayers around here. There are a whole fucking hell of a lot of pack members. That isn't a war you want to start."

I eyed Jay. "Wait, just how high up in your pack are you?"

Romeo blinked. "Seriously? You don't know?"

I shook my head. "Jay doesn't exactly share a lot with me about that side of his life."

"Let it rest, Romeo," said Jay, his hand moving to mine. "Gina, please agree to come home with me tonight. Actually, agree to stay until this blows over. If you refuse, Exavier will send someone to get you, and take you to stay with them."

"You're all acting like I'm some fragile doll who breaks easily," I returned.

"What the hell is your deal?" he snapped at me. "Why can't you just shut up and listen for once?"

14

I BLINKED UP AT HIM.

He paused. "Shit."

"I'm sorry, but I skipped the how-to-obey-your-dickheaded-shifter-boyfriend day at how-to-be-a-doormat school training," I shot back, my posture rigid in the seat.

Romeo pursed his lips. "I think he just wants to know you're safe."

"Stay out of this," said Jay harshly.

I elbowed him. "Be nice."

He leveled a hard look on me.

I grinned. "What?"

"You're a handful," he said.

"You love that about me." I nudged him lightly.

"I do." Jay tipped his head. "Hey, you called me your boyfriend."

I cringed when I realized he was right. "I also called you a dickhead. Want to get excited about that too?"

Romeo took another fry, seeming very amused by our back and forth.

I glanced at Jay and then paused. "You know you can't lock me away in your house forever, right? I mean, you get my job is to protect innocents."

He closed his eyes a moment and nodded. "I get it. I do, but give me this. Plus, I know you're hiding something from me. Don't make me have Romeo figure out what that something is."

"Dickhead."

"We already established that." Jay slid his hand through mine and squeezed it gently. "You'll stay with me until we get a better handle on this?"

"Jay, I know you think evil won't come at you at your place, but having me there is like painting a target on yourself. I'll be fine at my apartment."

Romeo snorted. "Tell her why whoever is

doing this would be super stupid to come to *your* home."

"I get Jay is a badass shifter," I said with all seriousness. "But he doesn't need to borrow my trouble. And really, if this is killing slayers, why wouldn't it go for fringe members of the pack here?"

"Fringe members?" echoed Romeo with a snort. "Jay. Trust me, if you don't, this won't go in the direction you want."

Jay grunted and then exhaled slowly, his hand still encasing mine. "Gina, I'm not a fringe member."

My eyes widened. "Tell me you didn't go rogue. Jayson!"

Romeo laughed more. "This is killing me. I should be recording it."

"Fuck off," snapped Jay before looking at me. His gaze darted away. "I'm kind of high up in the local pack here."

"It's a huge pack. What are you? Are you their version of law enforcement too? So you like, do the job in real life *and* pack life?"

Jay swallowed hard. "Well, I do enforce things."

"Dear gods above, if anyone else in the

pack saw this right now, they'd try to challenge you for the chance to lead," said Romeo, snickering more. "Just tell the woman the truth."

As Romeo's words moved over me, I gasped, jerking my hand free from Jay's. "Why would someone need to challenge you to lead the pack? I get there are a fair number of alpha males within the pack, but they'd challenge the head alpha. The pack leader. The supreme badass."

Romeo laughed more. "Our supreme badass is currently tongue-tied around you."

Jay was the head alpha of the local pack? The actual top wolf, not just one of the many alpha males under the main guy?

The pack had always been secretive about its members and their rankings within it, but I never thought they'd be so secretive as to keep something as massive as Jay being the guy in charge. More than that, I never thought Jay would hide that from me. The knowledge that he had stung, though I couldn't explain why exactly. All I knew was, it caused me pain. As if he didn't trust me.

My shoulders slumped. "I see."

"Gina," said Jay, trying to take my hand in his once more.

I didn't let him.

He touched my chin, forcing me to face him. "You're pissed."

"No," I confessed, feeling deflated.

"She's hurt," said Romeo. "She believes you don't trust her and that's why you never told her the truth."

I glared at him. "What are you, his emotional radar?"

"In a sense. I'm one of his head advisors and part of his personal team of guards. My empath abilities help Jay lead."

Jay touched my arm lightly. "Gina."

"Did you think because I'm a slayer that I'd betray you? That I'd leak that information to Zachariah and an attempt would be made on you?"

"He knows full well who and what I am," he stated evenly. "I made the decision to keep the truth from you because…"

He didn't finish, and I had to wonder if *he* even knew the real reason.

I snorted and pushed my plate of food away from me, my appetite gone.

Romeo sighed. "Gina, you need to understand why packs do their best to hide the truth of who is who to anyone non-pack. If someone wanted to hurt the head of the pack, but they knew they couldn't physically beat him in a fight, who would they go after first?"

I shrugged. "His mate or his family, if he has one."

Romeo lifted his brows as if that explained everything.

I stared harder at him. "Jay isn't mated. Wait—he's not mated, right?"

"No," said Jay. "I'm not mated yet. I would have told you if I was."

"Yet?" I echoed, locking gazes with him. "And let's be honest. It was a legit question, seeing as how you never mentioned you were in charge of the pack."

He looked as if he could see into my soul. With the backs of his fingers, he touched my cheek. "Anyone who knows the truth is always at risk. And it's against pack policy to tell non-pack anything about our inner workings."

"Lindsay knows, doesn't she?"

He nodded and sighed. "But she only learned the truth *after* she mated Exavier.

When I was, uh, seeing her, I kept it from her."

"Pack politics are fucking stupid," I said, meaning every word of it.

Romeo laughed. "I agree. But, you should know why Jay is desperate to keep *you* near him right now."

"Romeo, no," said Jay, the command clear and left hanging there. "She isn't ready to hear the truth."

I snapped my fingers at Romeo. "Ignore him. Tell me why. Tell me this truth I'm not ready to hear."

"Gina," said Jay sternly.

I eyed him sideways. "Dude, you aren't my alpha. Don't go barking at me. I'll put you in a kennel and get you out later to let you pee, nothing more."

Romeo laughed softly and then cleared his throat.

Jay looked tired, but he nodded. "Gina, it's important that you stay close to me during this because I can protect you. My position can protect you. The pack will pull together to see to your safety in this, and Romeo is right. Anyone foolish enough to attack my home is waging war with the pack. He's also right in the fact that slayers are few here, pack is not."

Confused, I stared between the men. "Why would the pack protect me? I'm a slayer. There's still a lot of bad blood between shifters and slayers. I get that. I do."

"Gina," said Romeo.

"Romeo," Jay warned again.

I thought harder about it all and then lifted a brow. "People think I'm Jay's plus one?"

Romeo nodded. "Yes, and that thought will be cemented when Jay puts you under his protection."

I laughed so hard I hiccupped. "And the pack will believe that crap? I mean, I'm just Jay's friend. We're not in a relationship. We've never done the dirty deed, and while he's abstained from sex for over six months, he was pretty much a total man-whore before that. Oh, and I'm just a slayer. I think the ruse that I'm his plus one won't hold much water, but thanks for thinking it would. I appreciate the offer of protection, but save that card for your actual mate."

Romeo widened his eyes in Jay's direction

and made a face, like he was trying to get Jay to say something to me.

Jay grunted.

Romeo shrugged. "Fine. Remember this moment then. When she winds up dead because you couldn't tell her the truth, then you'll have only yourself to blame. Dumbass."

"Have a lot of respect for your alpha?" I mused.

Romeo grunted. "At the moment, no."

Jay slammed his fist on the table, making the drinks nearly spill. He then looked at me, his nostrils flaring. "You're not just a slayer. You said it yourself. Your father is a shifter who can wield magik. Guess what, sweetheart, that totally makes you fair game in the world of mates. From what Exavier told me, your title as a slayer gave my shifter side problems recognizing what was before me. He said it caused my animal side to manipulate my human side, making the human side of me behave questionably."

"Otherwise known as banging endless chicks, trying to fill a void," said Romeo under a fake cough that did nothing but draw more attention to his words.

Jay cleared his throat.

Everyone fell silent.

I was about to flip him off and leave when it all clicked. Gasping, I jerked around to face him, paling as I did. "You *really* think I'm your plus one?"

"I need for you to be serious here," he said, sounding raw. "Gina, I don't think you are. I *know* you are. And baby, I got confirmation from more than one source that I trust fully. Exavier is one of them. And think about Zachariah, and his rantings in and out of French. About how you thought he was confused by mixing up my name with your mate. He knows it too, Gina."

I raked my gaze over his hard body and shook my head. "You're broken, dude. Get your head checked and then pull it out of your ass. I'm not your mate. Slayers *don't* have mates."

"But you're not a normal slayer, are you?" asked Romeo. "Something else is in your mix, right?"

I tensed. "Son of a bitch. I'm not going to spend the rest of my life being bossed around by Jay. Not happening."

"Gina, enough," said Jay in a voice that made me want to obey him.

I stilled for a second, and then elbowed him hard. "Kiss my ass."

A wicked smile came over his face. "Gladly."

"Jay—"

He leaned close, inhaling deep. "Your scent drives me wild, Gina. Every time I'm around you, I want to pin you to the ground, mount you, and fuck you until I bathe your womb in my seed."

Romeo whistled and leaned back in the booth.

I merely sat there, my mouth agape, staring at Jay, unsure how to process what he'd just said. The idea of Jay pushing into me and exploding had a lot of merit. So much so that cream began to pool between my legs and I groaned, knowing the shifters in the booth with me could smell it with ease.

Jay's lips twitched, and he draped an arm around my shoulders, pulling me closer to him. "Soon."

"Not here though," Romeo said to Jay, giving him a stern look. "We should probably contact the rest of the pack and get her back to your house."

"Yes," said Jay, tugging me tighter against his body.

I pushed him to gain my freedom. "You've got a screw loose right now on your shifter side. When it's better, you'll laugh at how ridiculous this all is."

Romeo put a hand up, stopping Jay's protest on his lips. "She needs time."

"Someone is hunting her kind. We don't have time for her to fuck around and come to terms with this. The sooner I claim her, the sooner she gets the full backing and protection of the entire pack. And the sooner I'll always be able to track her, always sense if she's in danger, and I'll be able to heal her. I can't now. Romeo, every time she gets hurt, I sit by her bedside, hating myself for not doing what nature intended. I hunt those who hurt her, but it's not enough. It's never enough!"

Twisting in the booth, I cupped Jay's face, forcing him to look at me. "Jayson, stop. You don't have to hunt things for me."

"I do."

"Are you always this obstinate?"

He locked gazes with me—then everything around us slowed as he kissed me. His tongue eased around mine, and I moaned into his mouth. He took the kiss to another level, and when I realized I was about to beg the man to fuck me in a diner full of people, I gasped and jerked back from him, my fingers going to my swollen lips.

I blinked in surprise. "Jay?"

"I get you need time to process who we are to each other and that you're in deep denial, but Gina, I need you close to me right now. I won't be able to function if you're away from me when I know slayers are being targeted—when I know you're in danger. Please. For me, set aside your stubborn side and agree to stay at my place."

"Okay, but no bossing me around when I'm there," I said sternly.

He grinned.

I paused, thinking about our kiss. "Jay, I won't be another notch on your bedpost. You know that, right?"

Romeo laughed. "Oh, he more than knows that, Gina."

"Can you take me to my place so I can pack a bag?" I asked.

Jay laced his fingers through mine. "I'll buy you everything you need."

I snorted. "Uh, thanks, but I know cops aren't paid enough for what they do. No way am I letting you blow money on me."

Romeo lost it, laughing hard. "Dude, she has no clue what your net worth is, does she?"

Jay blushed. "Uh, no."

I thought about his home. It was huge and a fixer-upper. I'd always assumed he'd gotten it at a deep discount and was planning to fix it up slowly and then resell it. I also thought about how it seemed like he didn't actually live there. The more I thought about it, the more I glared at him. "Do not tell me you're one of those rich guys who likes projects. Who likes to fix broken things in their spare time? That isn't your actual home we've spent time in, is it, Jayson?"

He bit his lower lip. "It's not."

I stilled. "Jay, I'm not a project. I'm not that broken."

He lifted our joined hands. "I know, baby."

.

15

JAYSON BROUGHT THE MOTORCYCLE TO A STOP IN front of a giant house. It was the biggest home I'd ever been close to and had to have cost millions.

I took the helmet off and simply soaked in the sight before me. I eased off the back of the bike, refusing to believe what I strongly suspected to be true.

This was Jay's actual house.

Jay slid off his bike and put his hand out to me.

I stared at his hand and put mine on my hip, looking up at the home. "I've seen the pack house. This isn't it."

"No, it's not the pack house. I conduct business there and use it as a safe haven for pack wolves to live if they want or need to, and to house guest packs." He kept his hand out to me.

"This is your personal house?" I asked, refusing to take his hand.

He inclined his head.

"I see."

"Gina, what's wrong?"

Pushing my hair behind my ears, I pressed my lips into a thin line. "Just feeling like a fool. I opened up a lot to you in the last several months. I thought you were opening up to me too. I see the truth now."

Jay put his hand down and nodded his head towards the house. He led me in the direction of a side entrance.

A tall man stepped out of the door, wearing a dress shirt and slacks. He grinned as Jay tossed him his motorcycle keys. The man never said a word as he went to move Jay's bike.

Headlights splashed over the drive behind us.

I turned to see Romeo getting out of his sport's car. He tossed his keys to the other guy too, and then jogged up next to me.

I kept my lips pressed together tight.

His gaze flickered to Jay. "Well, at least you'll know she isn't with you for your money."

"*She i*sn't with *him* at all," I snapped, still hurt at the number of things Jay had kept from me for so long.

Romeo put his hand on my forearm. "Gina, how could he explain all this to you and still keep you protected from his enemies? He couldn't very well bring you home with him. You'd know right away that this is something a cop couldn't afford. To explain the house, he'd have to explain who he is to the pack. Who his family has been to this pack for as far back as we can trace our roots."

I shot Jay a look.

He cringed.

"You could have told me. I'd have still called you a dickhead," I said, my hurt lessening slightly.

The corner of his mouth drew up. "I've no doubt of that, Fiery One."

This time, when he put his hand out again, I took it, but I didn't budge. Instead, I tugged him. "How do you run the pack, work at the police station, and find time to renovate an old house, all while spending time with me?"

A displeased snort came from Romeo. "He doesn't need to work at all. He's big into making sure he's giving back. Plus, I think he likes a slice of his life to be somewhat normal. Though, Jay, Taylor, and I handle all the supernatural shit that comes through the station."

I bit my lower lip. "Correction, you and Jay do. From what I've heard, Taylor doesn't handle anything. In fact, I'm not sure he's even real."

Romeo laughed softly. "He's flighty like that. We blame the fact that he's a vampire."

I squeezed Jay's hand. "None of that answers how you find time for everything."

Jay didn't respond.

Romeo did. "He makes his own schedule at work. People in the right places know who Jay is and what he really does. They're happy to have his help at all, even if it's limited. Since I go where Jay goes, the same deal applies to me. The pack, even with as big as it is, goes smoothly and doesn't require a ton of his time. That's a mark of how great an alpha he is. Not all packs are like ours. Some have nothing but drama. As for the house and fixing it up—he bought the thing years ago with the intent of channeling his excess energy. He didn't get serious about it until you started spending time with him."

Jay growled ever so slightly. "Enough sharing."

I bumped hips with him. "Hush, I want to hear what he has to say."

Romeo sighed. "Gina, you should know that Jay's run on limited sleep for about six months now. I've told him it's not healthy. I told him that it could leave him vulnerable to his enemies, but he doesn't care."

I glanced between the men, a sinking feeling coming over me. "He isn't sleeping much because of me, is he?"

"Gina," said Jay.

I ignored him, focusing fully on Romeo. "Because he's taking time to hunt anything that's hurt me. And because he's taking time to spend with me when he should be sleeping."

Jay tugged on my hand. "How do you know I hunt things that hurt you?"

"I might have opened the file you have on me in your computer," I confessed, less proud of my hacking skills than I'd been during the act.

A question formed on his face. "The folder was password protected."

"I know. And before you yell at me about it, you need to understand that I don't require a cleanup crew to run behind me. Yes, I get hurt sometimes. It's an occupational hazard. One you run into with your work too. You've spent the last six months doubting my abilities and treating me like I'm some delicate porcelain doll that will be smashed to bits if I don't have you near me."

He huffed. "I'm not that bad."

Romeo cleared his throat.

Jay shot the man a hard look. "I'm not."

"You're right. You're worse," added Romeo. "You've had how many men watching over her when she's on patrol?"

My gaze whipped to Jay.

He had the decency to look slightly ashamed. "What? I worry."

"Just how many men are we talking?" I questioned.

"Way more than one." Romeo wagged his brows.

"You can stop helping now," pressed Jay.

Romeo grinned. "Yes, I could, but I won't."

"Jayson, you can't run yourself down for me. What if something big goes down? You could be hurt because you're not taking care of yourself."

"Is now a bad time to mention he's not gone on one weekend trip to the cabins we own in the woods? The pack has various cabins up there so we have an out-of-the-way place to shift and run free. If we don't do it on a regular basis, we can end up with some massive control issues." Romeo glanced at Jay. "He doesn't leave the city now because I think he's afraid something will happen to you, not to mention he doesn't want to miss out on time with you."

I squeezed Jay's hand tightly. "Jayson!"

Romeo let out a long breath. "I knew he had it bad for a woman. I knew she was redheaded and I knew she was a slayer. But he locked down the rest from me, and the men he'd tasked with following you were told it was because Jay wanted to keep tabs on the slayers, just in case there was an issue. And while he kept secrets from you about the pack and who he is, he kept just as many secrets from us about *you*. I think he was worried how we'd take the news."

Jay drew me to him. "I still need to tell the pack, baby."

"Tell them what?" I asked. "Why do they

need to be told anything about me?"

Romeo touched my shoulder. "You're his plus one, Gina. He needs to make that clear to the pack. He can't risk one of them hurting you, thinking they're protecting their alpha. Jay would lose his shit—and trust me when I say that is not something anyone wants to have happen."

I pressed myself to Jay's side. "You're going to sleep tonight if I have to club you over the head, knock you out, and force it to happen. If you think I won't, you don't know me very well."

Romeo beamed. "She's perfect for you, Jay."

"I know. Now we just have to convince *her* of that," said Jay with a nod.

Romeo wore a smug expression as he followed close behind us when Jay opened the side door. We entered the home, and my jaw dropped. I was only six feet in and already I knew the place should have been showcased on the front of a magazine. "Jayson!"

He offered a sheepish smile. "Yes?"

"You are never, ever allowed to come over to my apartment if this is what you like." I wasn't joking. I lived in a small one-bedroom apartment painted institution white on every wall. I had one loveseat that had never actually been sat on, a barstool that sat under the two-foot ledge in the cutout between the galley kitchen and living room, and a bed. That was it. I was a no-frills kind of girl when it came to my place.

Jay would never make it at my place.

And I didn't make a habit of inviting anyone over.

He walked me into the biggest kitchen I'd ever seen.

Two men entered, all smiles until they saw me with him. The men all stared at each other, and I stiffened, realizing the men were shifters and they were all communicating mentally.

One's eyes widened as he stared at me and then Jay.

My guess was, Jay just let them know I was a slayer. That or they smelled it on me.

Romeo rubbed my shoulders. "Relax. It's fine."

Easy for him to say. He was one of them. I was something that killed their kind when it was called for. Somehow, I didn't think a welcome mat would be rolled out anytime soon.

Jay eased me closer to him. "We'll hunker

down here. It's safer than being out there right now. Once we get a better handle on what's happening, we'll make our next move."

I glanced at the shifter males just as four more entered the kitchen. "Is it really safer here for me?"

Jay turned and dipped his head, his lips close to mine. "It is."

Believing him was difficult, especially with the way the newcomers narrowed their gazes on me.

Romeo only drove my point home when he eased himself out from behind us and planted his body between the men who had just entered the kitchen and me. Yeah. Sure felt nice and safe — compared to the vampire club, it probably was.

Not really an upsell.

Jay growled lightly and shot a look at the men, as if warning them, before he continued to lead me through the home.

We were almost to the grand staircase when a man I knew well walked out from a long hallway. I'd spent three years of my life with him, and then everything had ended in an instant. I'd not seen him since the day we'd parted ways.

16

MY MIND RACED, SURE I'D GONE MAD. SAMUEL couldn't be standing in Jay's home. What business would he have with the pack and how the hell did he even know Jay? None of it made any sense, yet there he was, plain as day—the man I'd spent three years of my life with. And the man who'd broken my heart.

His black hair was shorter than I remembered but still to his chin. He had a cell phone in his hand and he held it low, reading the screen. He stood as tall as Jay and actually looked a great deal like him, now that I saw them in the same room.

I couldn't move or breathe. I let go of Jay's hand.

Jay tried to get me to walk, but my feet

remained in place as my heart pounded in my chest madly. Part of me wanted to cry. Another part wanted to shout at Samuel for what he'd put me through. I did neither. I just stared at him. "Gina?"

Samuel stiffened and looked up slowly, his dark brown eyes widening as he spotted me. Confusion flashed through his eyes. "Regina?"

I bit my lower lip, my body frozen in place, my mind still racing.

He dropped the phone and rushed me, lifting me in his arms. No words were spoken as his lips found mine. I didn't return the kiss. I pretty much just stared wide-eyed, trying to wrap my head around why Samuel was at Jay's house. And I was still torn between crying and yelling.

He walked while holding me before pressing me against the wall, still pressing his lips to mine. Within seconds, his hands were high on my thighs, his fingertips just under my cutoff jean shorts. I pushed at his hands to get him to stop.

It took me a second to realize someone was growling loudly while others were shouting.

"Samuel! Knock it off! We can't hold him much longer!"

"Put her down, Samuel! Jay is losing his shit," said another.

Pushing his hands away and moving my face to break the kiss, I locked gazes with him. "Sam?"

He tried to kiss me again, apparently unconcerned with the fact the other guys were still shouting at him. I dodged the kiss, tearing up.

Guess crying was going to win out.

He stared at me, wide-eyed. "Regina, hon, I couldn't find you. I looked everywhere. I hired someone to try to find you, even. I realized about five minutes after we said good-bye that it was the wrong move. I came back looking for you, trying to make it right, but you'd vanished," he said, touching my lips. "Wait. Why are you here?"

The pain he'd put me through back then filled my chest and I couldn't help but shed a tear. I didn't like showing weaknesses or feeing vulnerable. He made me feel both. I wiggled to get down, but he didn't let me. "Put me down."

"Tell me why you're here," he said, keeping me where I was.

"Jay brought me," I said.

Samuel stiffened and set me down slowly, keeping himself in front of me as he turned to look at the sizable crowd we'd gathered.

As I peeked around him, I spotted at least a dozen men there, a chunk of them pinning Jay to the expensive marble floor, the others ready to grab Samuel if the need arose.

Jay snarled, his eyes amber, his teeth that of the wolf. He strained against the men pinning him down. "Get off me!"

A guy in a red shirt locked gazes with Samuel. "Are you fucking nuts? You do *not* make out with Jay's woman!"

Samuel spun to look at me. "You're *with* Jay?"

"As his friend, mostly. Okay, maybe more than a friend. I'm still unsure."

"Hear the noise he's making? It's one a shifter male makes when he wants to protect *his* woman. It's instinctual, Gina. So, I'll ask again. Are you *with* Jay?" questioned Samuel snidely.

I felt like I was being asked to pick between the two. As if my answer was vitally important. "He's very important to me. His wires are a little crossed. He thinks I'm his plus one. I've tried explaining I'm more than likely not. I mean maybe I am, but I don't know. I do know he's stubborn."

Romeo was suddenly there, moving closer to me, as if to protect me. "She's Jay's mate. She just doesn't quite believe us on that fact yet. And correction—they're *both* stubborn."

Samuel backed up, wiping his hands over his face. "Fuck."

I tried to go to him, to calm him down, but Romeo held me back.

Samuel spun and punched the wall, not that far from where I was standing.

I actually jolted as he did, surprised to see a side to him that involved violence. He'd been nothing but sweet and tender when I was with him.

Romeo growled, throwing himself against me, pushing me back from Samuel and the others. He then turned, keeping me behind him. While I knew he was trying to protect me, I couldn't help but feel it was yet another example of a man thinking I couldn't handle myself.

Jay roared, and the men on him were bucked off like they were barely there. The next thing I knew, Jay was charging Samuel.

Samuel growled, and I knew a fight was about to happen. They collided and began going at one another. The other men tried to tear them apart, but nothing they did worked. The pair fell over a table that had what looked to be an expensive vase on it. Another of the men caught the vase before it would have hit the floor, but the table was a lost cause.

Jay and Samuel kept going and the other men stepped back, as if they'd realized there was no breaking the two apart.

The idea of Jay and Samuel hurting one another made me sick to my stomach. Without thinking, I darted around Romeo and ran into the fray, pushing in between Jay and Sam. I shoved each of them hard as I drew on my slayer skills. I thrust them apart.

Sam tried to make a move at Jay again, and I shoved Sam hard enough to send him falling backwards.

I looked up at Jay, and while I wanted to be angry about his temper, I knew deep down that it hurt him to see Samuel kiss me, despite me not returning the kiss. Still, it didn't make it okay for Jay to attack a human. He could kill Samuel with ease. "Jay, enough!"

The amber faded from his eyes and his mouth returned to normal. "You're telling me *enough*, Gina? He fucking kisses you in *my* home, in front of me, but you're yelling at me? Really?"

"You can't attack Sam. He's human and you could kill him without—" I thought about it harder. My gaze whipped to Samuel. "You're a shifter?"

He flinched and averted his gaze, calming instantly. "Yes."

"Not once in three years did you think to bring that up to me?" I asked, wanting to punch him myself and save Jay the time. "I told you the truth about me, and you let me sit there and spill my guts, but you never once said, 'hey, I'm a wolf shifter'?"

Jay growled. "*He's* your Sam? The guy you were with for three years?"

His men grabbed him again, pushing him back from me.

I lowered my gaze, hating that this was hurting him. "Yes. Sorry."

Jay snarled. "You screwed my cousin! For three years!"

Putting a hand on my hip, I rounded on

him, my finger going to his chest as I jabbed him. "And how many other women have you been with?" I asked, in a voice that said I wasn't playing around. It wasn't as if he didn't have things in his past that he wished he could change. "And correct me if I'm wrong, but weren't you also sticking it to my best friend, Jayson?"

"He's blood, Gina!" he shouted, as if that made all the difference in the world. As much as I knew this caused him pain, it didn't give him the right to yell at me. He wasn't a saint by any means.

"So?" I shot back.

He blinked. "So?"

I nodded. "Yeah. So what? Lindsay is like a sister to me. Didn't stop you, did it? So, yes, so the fuck what? Sam and I were a couple. It's history now. Just like you and Lindsay. So get it over it, dickhead."

He blinked.

I didn't stop. "Want to keep going on this or are you ready to dump the macho, alpha-man bullshit? Stop trying to piss on my leg and stop growling all the time, it's annoying."

Jay looked like he was going to say something but was at a loss for words.

My focus went to Sam. "Why didn't you tell me the truth? It wouldn't have changed how I felt about you."

"Because my alpha had forbidden any of us from revealing what we are," he said, his gaze flickering to Jay. "I thought you'd sense it on me, but you never did. I don't know why. I was just happy you let me be part of your life."

I glanced at Jay. "Jayson is big on keeping things from people he cares about. Like the fact he's the pack's *head* alpha and he's apparently Richie Fucking Rich, so I shouldn't be too surprised he ordered you to keep a secret from someone you cared about too."

Again, Jay said nothing, looking thunderstruck.

My attention returned to Sam. "When you walked out the door, I left too. It hurt, a lot, for a long time…but I got over it. I'm not that person anymore, Samuel. In all honesty, you're part of the reason why I stopped letting men into my heart. Why I'm afraid to trust Jay fully."

There, I'd said it. It didn't taste great going down, but it at least went.

Samuel closed his eyes a moment. "Regina, I'm serious. I came back five minutes later, wanting us to be together. I knew I'd made a mistake."

That night was still fresh in my mind. The emotions were still raw, and I couldn't go down that road again. "The fact you left at all is the problem, Sam. I would have never done that to you. You had the power to hurt me, and you did. A lot."

Jay grumbled.

I ignored him, focusing on Samuel instead. "That being said, I want to know how you've been. What you've been doing. Did you ever find that perfect person you were searching for, the one who was ready to settle down, and try to have a family?"

"No," he said, his voice low. "I'd had plans for that with you, but I knew you weren't my mate, and I wasn't sure how the pack would handle me being with you—a slayer."

Romeo groaned. "And this just managed to get worse. Really, Samuel, you didn't need to bring up wanting to marry her in front of Jay."

I pointed at Romeo. "Why not? You'd just tell Jay about it later. Look, time saved."

Romeo's lips twitched before he laughed. "You do realize you're perfect for our alpha, right? And somehow, you're scarier than him, and you're only like this high." He put his hand up to his chin.

"Tall enough to kick you in the nads," I said, eyeing his family jewels before I grinned and wiped my cheeks.

He cupped himself. "Samuel, you are on your own here."

Samuel watched me. "Jay's going to fucking kill me already, and I can't get any *more* dead. So, I'm going to tell you that I've missed you so much."

"I miss our friendship," I said, my stomach tight. "You were my everything back then, and it all ended in the blink of an eye."

"Samuel," Jay ground out.

Samuel glanced downwards. "I'm sorry. I was close to turning my back on the pack to be with you, Regina, and I knew you weren't ready for marriage yet. Our age difference left us at different places in our lives. I walked out, intending to return to the pack, but then I realized you were worth going rogue. But you were gone and, Regina, you *really* know how to stay off the grid. I've missed you, and I want to spend time with you too. But Jay won't let that happen."

"Sam, I would love to have coffee with you and catch up. To be clear, I don't want to go down relationship memory road or re-kindle what was there, but I do want to know how you're doing. Plus, the more Jay acts like an ass, the more I want to give you a hand job." I winked.

Samuel coughed, his eyes wide.

"Gina!" shouted Jay.

"Oh, look, now I feel like blowing you, Sam. Think dumbass is going to keep going until you get anal?" I asked with a grin that said I was joking.

Sam's lips twitched, because he knew my warped sense of humor well. "Knowing Jay? Yes. Hell, I'll get twenty-four-hour access to you with as bad as his temper is."

Grunting, Jay shook the men off him and came toward me. "I'm sorry. Please don't blow my cousin."

It was nearly impossible to avoid laughing.

Most of the men around us failed.

Romeo made no move to hide his laughter.

He put a hand on the wall to support himself as he shook.

Jay dragged me into his arms and hugged me to him.

Putting my head to his chest, I returned his embrace. "You better?"

"I am." He pushed my hair over my shoulders. "Gina, what if I have some food and drinks sent upstairs? We can get cleaned up and maybe watch a movie or something until we're ready to get some sleep?"

I lifted a brow. "This is a ploy to keep me away from Sam, isn't it?"

"Partly," he admitted. "The other part is, we need time together. Just us."

"Okay, but we should bring your walking mood ring," I pointed at Romeo, "because you have two outward settings. Funny and dickhead. He can decode your alpha-ness for me."

The men laughed softly.

Jay winked. "I think we can manage without Romeo in the room with us."

I glanced at Romeo. "I need you on speed dial."

Romeo snorted. "He'll behave."

"He better."

Jay touched my chin again. "That plan work for you? I particularly like it because it doesn't involve you giving my cousin a hand job."

I pressed my lips together. "I don't know. It's hard to *beat* that."

Laughing, Jay bent and lifted me, putting me over his right shoulder. "Let's go, Fiery One, before you unman me any more in front of the guys."

I lifted my head and moved the veil of red hair hanging in my face. "Nice to meet you all. Sam, we'll talk soon! Romeo, I'll see you in about five minutes."

Samuel watched Jay carrying me away and I couldn't help but feel bad when I noticed the sad look in his eyes.

17

JAY HURRIED UP THE STAIRS AND DOWN A LONG hallway to the room at the end. He opened the door, carried me in, and then turned, shutting and locking the door behind him. He took me to the bed and plopped me down on it.

I looked around the room. It was massive. More than any one person needed. The bed was larger than a king-size. I wasn't even sure how it could be that big, but it was. A set of French doors was directly across from the bedroom entrance. Moonlight spilled in through them, making a multitude of squares appear on the hardwood floor.

"Jay, this room is huge. It's like five times the size of my apartment."

He walked to one of the four doors, not

counting the one in and out of the room. "Baby, you can get cleaned up in here. I'll have everything you'll need brought up. You're what? A size four?"

I sat up on the bed and eyed him. "Why? And no, I'm a six."

"You sure?" he asked, looking me over. "There isn't much to you."

I eased off the bed and walked past him into the bathroom. I came to a dead stop. "Jayson, the bathroom is also way bigger than my entire apartment. That bathtub looks like it will fit at least four people." I spun and grabbed his hand. "Come on, let's see if it fits two comfortably."

Jay gasped. "Gina, you're kidding, right? You don't want to take a bath with me."

I bounced up and down. "I'm excited. Let's do it."

"Do it?" He tugged at the collar of his T-shirt.

"Yes, let's take a bath together." As I said it, I realized how crazy it sounded. It had sort of flown out without me thinking. But, there was no denying it was what I wanted to do. I found myself starting the bath water, really hoping Jay would agree to the idea of testing it out with me.

He took a deep breath. "That might be pushing my control levels around you past the edge. By the end of the bath, you'd be a claimed woman. And since you're still in denial about who you are to me, that could present a problem if my wife refuses to believe she is, indeed, my wife."

My hand found his. "How do you know that I'm your mate?"

"I've known since the minute I first saw you, but my wolf was confused as hell. I sought out relief but didn't find any. Then, right after Lindsay and Exavier were mated, without my knowledge, Exavier had a talk with some higher-ups who I'm guessing hold a lot of power, and they set my wolf straight. It was then I knew with all my heart who you are to me."

I avoided looking at him. "How do *I* know?"

"I wish I could answer that for you, baby." He leaned against the bathroom doorframe.

My hand went to where I'd been bitten by Reynaud. The urge to tell Jay the truth slammed into me with a force I didn't even bother to attempt to understand. Shutting the water off, I sat on the edge of the tub and pulled off my outer shirt and then my T-shirt. I kicked off my shoes. I was left in a small black tank top and my shorts.

"Jay, can you promise to not wolf out or anything if I tell you something?"

"I can promise to try my best to keep it under control," he said.

Turning while still sitting on the edge of the tub, I moved my hair to show him what Reynaud had done to me.

His gaze narrowed, and he was suddenly in front of me, kneeling. His fingers went to the bite mark that Reynaud hadn't healed over for me. "This is not that old."

My hand went to his. "It happened the night we were at the club. Afterwards. After you got called into work. I got to my Jeep, left, and was only three blocks away when my tire blew. My guess is they had something to do with that."

His body coiled with rage but when he looked at me, his eyes held only flecks of amber. An indication he was really trying to keep his beast at bay. "The master vampire?"

Nodding, I squeezed his hand. "The three vamps who were standing outside of the private room that night appeared, along with around twenty buddies. I wasn't carrying any weapons, so I used my heels and a tire iron to kill them."

He lifted a brow.

"Then I felt this horrible darkness move up my legs and body, locking me in place. I tried to move. I tried everything I could, but nothing worked, and then I saw him—the master vampire, Reynaud. He looked both amused and turned on by the fact I'd killed so many of his men. He actually told me there were more where they came from. And he wanted me to join him back at the club."

The softest of growls started in the back of Jay's throat. He held himself together.

"I could not get my body to respond to anything. I couldn't move, and his vamp mojo was working on me to a degree, making me want to be with him sexually. Making we want to surrender to him.

"He was there, holding me by my neck, and I thought he was going to kill me. He could have with ease. He didn't. He fed from me once and healed that wound over. He told me he could make me want him, make me give in."

I bit my lower lip. "If he'd have ordered me

to do just that, I think I would have, because I wouldn't have been able to stop his influence over me. And I think he would have done it if Zachariah and the others hadn't shown up when he did. Reynaud bit me again but he didn't heal this one, and it didn't want to heal over for the first day and a half after it all happened."

Jay snarled and rotated his head, much like an animal would, and the flecks of amber multiplied in his eyes.

"Zachariah had people from the med unit come to his house for me. They were worried about how much blood I was losing. Zachariah actually attempted to heal it himself, but it didn't work. He debated on calling you over to help in some way, but he was positive you'd launch a full-scale attack on the den, igniting a war between the vamps and shifters

"I kept drifting in and out of sleep," I said, drawing him closer so I could hug him. "Jayson, Reynaud was in my dreams. But I don't think they were just dreams. They felt real somehow."

Jay growled fully.

My hand went to his cheek. "I'm going to stop telling you everything if you keep losing it."

He drew me closer to him.

"In the dreams, he taunted me, knowing I couldn't fight back against him. And he kept telling me how he'd found a way to convert slayers into vampires, and he was 'most curious to know if he could do so with me.'"

Jay stood fast and went for the door. I ran in front of him and put my arms out, grabbing hold of each side of the doorframe. "Jayson, no!"

He snarled again, his eyes filling with amber. "He dies."

"He wants that. He knows what you are. I don't know how," I said, my emotions welling. "He wants to make you mad and draw you to him. He sees it as sport. And he told me he had the power to control your wolf. To make you hurt me. I don't know if that's true and I don't want to find out. Because I know I wouldn't hurt you—even if you lost control and hurt *me*."

"Move," he said, his voice barely under-standable.

"No."

"Regina, move," he said, using my whole name, something he rarely did.

I shook my head. "Reynaud is the reason

Zachariah freaked out and forced me to go on paid leave. And my guess is, he's behind the slayer deaths. I know what I'm capable of compared to the other slayers, and I couldn't stand against him. They never had a chance."

Jay tried to shove past me and nearly succeeded.

Drawing upon my extra strength, I pushed him back, but I did so too hard. He went back fast, and I tried to grab him. The next I knew Jay was tripping over the side of the tub and going in. I fell in on top of him. He came up, partially with me straddling him.

His eyes widened as the amber faded away. "Gina!"

Unable to help myself, I glanced around the tub, noting how much room was still left in it. "Well, now we know at least two people fit in this thing with a lot of room to spare."

Our gazes met.

Dipping my head, I kissed him. The kiss wasn't soft or gentle. It was needy and hungry. It was six months' worth of sexual tension coming to a head. There were far too many wet clothes between us. I tugged at his wet shirt but made no headway with it.

"Jayson," I pleaded.

He sat up straight in the tub, keeping me on his lap. He peeled off his shirt and my breath caught at the sight of his bare, wet chest. He lifted the bottom of my tank top and eased it up, moving it over my breasts slowly. He then pulled it over my head and had to work my hair out of it. Jay cupped my breasts and squeezed them gently, his mouth going to one of my nipples. I gasped and ground against him.

Growling, he stood, taking me with him as well. He set me on my feet in the tub, steadying me, before he bent and started peeling my jean shorts and panties down my body. I stepped out of them, putting a hand on his shoulder to keep from falling. He tossed them across the bathroom, and they made a wet slapping sound.

Jay then stayed bent before me in the tub. He kissed my hip bones to start with before trailing a line of kisses to my mound. He rubbed his face over the small strip of dark red hair I kept there. Glancing up at me, he grinned and waggled his brows.

I laughed as I remembered his offer to rub his facial hair on me, just like he was doing now.

When he parted my folds, I nearly lost my

footing and fell. His tongue eased over my swollen bud, and I gasped, pleasure building in me at a fast rate. He inserted a finger into me, and my body fought against it. The look on Jay's face was priceless. I thought he'd come then and there. I rode his finger, and he added a second one, working my body with an expert touch. Soon, I was accommodating him, and he went for a third. His tongue moved over my clit, and I lost it, my orgasm coming on hard and fast.

He stood, water streaming off his powerful frame. He kicked off his shoes. He undid his jeans and pulled them off, tossing them farther into the bathroom as well. He didn't have on underwear.

I found myself unable to look away from him. The man was a work of art. Need slammed through me, and I pushed on him, forcing him to sit in the tub again. I straddled him at once and captured his mouth with my lips.

He aligned his cock head with my wet entrance as our tongues stayed wrapped around each other. Jay pushed in slowly at first, and I moaned into his mouth.

The more we kissed, the more my body loosened around the girth of his cock. I eased down more on him, and he broke the kiss, thumping his head back against the tiled wall.

"G-Gina," he hissed as I continued to slide down his shaft.

I wasn't sure I could take any more and started to get nervous that his size was going to be an issue.

He arched up, driving into me deeper.

Crying out, I pushed on his chest and finally settled all the way onto him. I stayed there a moment, getting used to how full he made me. Then I began to move slowly on him. Leaning, my lips found his again, and we kissed with less aggression now, yet the kiss was still passionate. I continued to move on him.

He bit my lower lip gently, his hands on my hips. "Right there. Yeah, baby. Bounce. Just like that. Fuck yeah."

I did as he wanted and tensed as pleasure began to build deep in me. Something else started to build too, but I wasn't sure what it was. It felt like static. I ignored it and rode Jay's hard body harder and faster.

His eyes started to swirl with amber.

Instinctively, I caught his chin. "No, Jay. Tonight is you and me. Not the wolf."

He pumped up into me like a piston.

"Want to claim you," he said, sounding strained.

I locked gazes with him. "Give me tonight, Jayson. Please. Let it just be us."

Nodding, he closed his eyes and put his head back.

I knew it was for my benefit. To keep from biting me. And I appreciated the restraint he was showing. I moved my hips, making a figure eight pattern on him, and his hands shot to each side of the tub. Increasing my pace, the pleasure that had been building burst free from me. My pussy tightened around his cock and Jay lost it, ramming up and rooting in me as he came.

We both shook as we stayed like that, me on him, him clutching the sides of the massive tub.

He looked up at me and grinned. "My tool is so fucking happy it got to hammer you that I can't feel my lower half."

Laughing, I dipped my head and kissed him.

He wrapped his arms around me. "Mmm, that was so worth the wait. Can we do it again, like now?"

"I'm hungry."

He snorted. "You're always hungry, woman."

"Feed me and then fuck me more."

"This is a great plan," he said with a sexy grin. "Another feels like Christmas moment."

I eased off him, and then laughed when I looked at the bathroom, noting the puddles around various articles of clothing.

Jay stood and held my hand as I got out of the tub. He exited as well and grabbed towels for us, in addition to laying some out on the floor to try to soak up the excess water. Turning, he stared at me and a silly grin spread across his handsome face.

"What?" I asked, feeling self-conscious standing before him naked, despite the fact he was too.

"I've spent years picturing you naked." He put his towel over his shoulder, handing me mine as he did. "The image I had in my mind was one I didn't think could be improved upon. I was wrong. Very wrong."

I groaned and then smelled my hair. "Jay, I smell like a wet dog. And while I get that probably happens to you every time you go out in the rain, I'm not a fan of it on me."

He laughed.

"I need to wash my hair."

He glanced at the shower, then me. "I'm all for that. I should help. You have a lot of hair."

"If we get in the shower together, there is zero chance my hair will get washed," I said, as I watched his cock harden while he stood there.

Jay stroked himself and continued to stare at me. In the next moment, he had me up and off my feet and was headed out of the bathroom, to the huge bed. I barely had time to wrap my mind around it before he had my legs spread and was thrusting into me once more. My legs wrapped around his waist and I clung to him as he kept going.

18

I STIRRED, MY MIND FOGGY FROM BEING PULLED from sleep. I found myself pinned to the bed by a muscular body from behind. Grinning, I eased back, seeking warmth from Jay.

Oddly, I found none. Whereas he was normally always slightly warmer than average, I'm guessing from his shifter side, he was cool to the touch now.

I shivered and reached down, grabbing the blankets and pulling them up our bodies. "You're freezing."

He ran a hand up my bare thigh, making me shiver more.

I laughed. "Ohmygod, you're making me even colder."

He chuckled lightly, moved my long and

thankfully washed hair to the side, baring my shoulder and neck to him. I kept my back pressed against his front and closed my eyes as he caressed my neck. He pressed his lips to it, and I felt the smallest of pinpricks.

Pleasure raced through me, and I arched my back into him. As I did, something growled from the foot of the bed.

I glanced down as Jay continued to bite my neck. What I saw confused me.

Jay was standing at the foot of the bed, his amber gaze locked on me, his nostrils flaring, his naked form partially covered in fur. His shoulders heaved and grew bigger as claws emerged from his fingertips.

"Jay?" I asked, unable to wrap my mind around how he could be in two places at once.

I tried to turn but found I was locked in place. Darkness crept over me slowly, starting at my feet and working its way up my body. I didn't need to be told who was behind me, and it wasn't Jay.

"Slayer," whispered Reynaud as he released my neck. He licked it then. "Did you think coming to him would keep me out of your dreams? Did you think your precious wolf could protect you?"

"Jayson!"

His growl deepened, and Reynaud lifted his hold on me enough for me to sit up. I did, and I faced the end of the bed. Jay was still there, changing more and more into a wolf.

"See what I can make him do?" said Reynaud, his weight vanishing from the bed.

The darkness remained…and brought with it fear.

I stared at Jay and realized his anger wasn't directed at Reynaud. It was focused all on me. I put my hands up and was about to attempt to reason with him when he snarled and leaped up and over the end of the bed.

I screamed his name a second before his shift was complete and he came down on me in full wolf form. The next thing I knew, he lunged for my throat.

19

SCREAMING, I CAME AWAKE FAST IN A COLD sweat, my hand on my neck, my heart racing. It took me a minute or two to realize I'd been dreaming. That Jay hadn't attacked me, and Reynaud had not been in bed with me.

That didn't calm my nerves.

I reached for Jay to find his side of the bed was empty. "Jayson?"

He didn't answer.

Moonlight streamed in through the large French doors that overlooked the pool and back-yard. I eased from the bed slowly and went to the pile of clothing that had been brought up with the food earlier. I grabbed a pair of black panties and a matching fitted tank top. I picked up a pair of pajama bottoms and stilled, realizing the darkness I'd felt in my dream was still in the air.

And it was still as strong as it had been in the dream.

I listened, trying to hear anything that might be off.

While I didn't hear anything, my inner alarms began to sound. The word "wolves" pulsed at me from within. Since I was in a house full of them, I didn't panic.

But when I sensed something near, stalking me, like a predator before a kill, I glanced around for something that could be used as a weapon, and found nothing.

Whatever was close wasn't Jay, but it was a wolf. More than one, even. As the darkness pulsed in the air around me, I realized it was playing a part in what was happening. It was influencing the wolves coming for me. Wolves who were part of Jay's pack. I didn't want to hurt them, especially knowing Reynaud was behind their actions, but I couldn't very well permit myself to be killed for the sake of being nice and having a heart.

If I remained in the room, there would be a fight. While I didn't know how many wolves were coming for me, I did know they'd leave me no choice but to fight back and possibly injure or kill one or more of them. To avoid that scenario from playing out, I looked for an exit.

My gaze snapped to the French doors. I moved towards them quietly, unconcerned that I was in only a tank top and panties. That was the least of my worries. Avoiding being left in a situation where it was kill or be killed with Jay's men was the top priority.

Slowly, I turned the knob on the door, and the door opened. There was the slightest of creaks from the hinges, and I stilled, hoping the wolves hadn't heard it.

There was a loud crashing sound behind me, and I knew that it was the bedroom door giving way.

So much for them not hearing it.

Turning and taking a fighting stance, I watched as a massive gray wolf leaped at me. I put my arms up to deflect it as it struck me with its full body weight. Normally, that wouldn't have been a huge issue, although it would have hurt. The fact I was standing near a second-floor balcony changed matters dramatically. One second, I was on the balcony, and the next, the fully shifted wolf and I were going over the stone banister.

My right shoulder struck something hard and unforgiving before I was suddenly under water. When I realized I was in the pool, under-water, with a gigantic wolf on me, I kicked at the beast, trying to put distance between it and myself. I managed to do just that and swam to the other side of the pool. I pushed out of the water and spun, sensing more wolves closing in on me.

The one in the pool struggled to get out of the water in fully shifted form. He was left doggie paddling in place. I couldn't worry about him at the moment. I had bigger issues.

I could sense at least two wolves creeping closer from my left and an undetermined number from my right.

A white one came rushing from the dark-ness, and I twisted, knocking it away from me, using the least amount of force I could.

It was quickly replaced by another gray one. This one chomped down as it came at me, catching my hand in the process. I ignored the pain and kicked the wolf away from me. I grabbed an end table from the poolside furniture. As another wolf attacked, I hit it with the table before running in the direction of the pool house.

20

I was nearly to one of the many French doors of the pool house when I was struck from behind, my body propelled forward. I crashed through a set of French doors, the glass breaking around me, cutting me in the process before I landed on the hard marble floor. I leaped to my feet and spun around in time to deflect the wolf, flipping it up and over me. It landed on the floor and snarled violently.

"Dude, I'm trying not to hurt you!" I yelled, but no one was home behind the vicious snarl.

It scrambled to its feet and came at me as three more jumped through the windows and doors.

"Shit." I turned and ran, everything happening in mere seconds. When I looked forward, I found an enormous gathering hall of sorts, filled with men. They all seemed to make a grab for me, not the fucking wolves trying to eat me.

To them, I was the enemy. Not their pack mates.

The next I knew, I had mind-melded wolves trying to kill me and guys in human form trying to take me on. I fought back as best I could, delivering non-lethal strikes.

Samuel and Romeo were suddenly there, thrusting the men back from me, shouting at them.

"Stop!" yelled Samuel. "She's Jay's woman!"

They either didn't hear him or they didn't care.

Romeo ushered me through the crowd at a fast rate, and when it cleared, I saw Jay standing there, face-to-face with a man who matched him in height and build. The same man I'd caught sight of outside the vampire club. The very one who helped save me from Reynaud. And the same one I'd seen outside the diner.

The man's black hair was long and pulled together loosely at his neck. He had a full beard, the type that seemed popular with men as of late. He turned his head, his green gaze finding me.

Jay looked horrified at what was happening before he began shouting at his pack.

I ran at Jay—but at the last second, felt the overwhelming need to go to the man with the green eyes, so I did.

He put his arms out and caught me, holding me in place.

I panted and pointed to the crowd. "Vampire influencing the shifted ones," I managed, partially out of breath. "Others just want to kill me for being me, I think."

Jay snarled and then turned to his men. He roared, and everyone but those shifted into wolf form stopped moving. "Restrain them!"

The men listened to Jay's command like God himself came down and issued the order. I clung to the guy with green eyes and watched the scene unfold. I then remembered the wolf in the pool.

My gaze met Samuel's. "Sam, in the pool! One's in the pool. I don't know if he can shift back to human form to get out. He knocked me off the balcony, and we fell into the pool together."

Samuel nodded as he and three other men ran from the pool house.

I stared around, trying to figure out if everyone was done trying to kill me.

Jay came at me, his eyes wide. "You're bleeding!"

He reached for me, and I threw myself at the man holding me as the dream about Jay biting my throat out hit me full force.

Jay drew up short and sniffed the air. "Baby, you're afraid of me? Why?"

"I'm not, it's just…I kind of need a moment here."

He looked past me at the man holding me. "Baby, will you let Romeo close to you? He can check your hand. And get you away from an alpha who charged into my territory, demanding a meeting with me and my pack at an ungodly hour."

I twisted in the man's arms.

His green gaze ran over me, and his brows met as confusion crossed his features. "Do I know you?"

I shook my head but then stopped. He did seem familiar, but I couldn't place him.

"Shaw," said Jay, his voice deep. "Release my woman."

A group of about twelve men surrounded Shaw as if to protect him. I realized then they must be from his pack. Several of them looked really familiar, but I couldn't place them.

Jay growled long and deep. "Get your hands off her!"

"Uh, let's all play nice," said Romeo, sounding as if he was trying to appear extra calm when he was anything but okay with what was going on. He put his hand out to me. "How about we step away from Shaw?"

"Is she going to start making out with him like she did Samuel?" asked someone from the crowd.

Another laughed. "Nah, she'll just offer to give the guy a hand job to piss Jay off more."

As the words left the man's mouth, Shaw snarled, pushed me behind him and pointed at the men who had spoken. "Do nae talk of her in that manner again! If you do, I'll rip yer fucking tongues from yer heads. Am I clear?"

Stunned, I stared at his back, wondering why he'd taken the comments so personally.

There was certainly something that felt safe and right about him, but that didn't mean much.

In the next breath, Shaw was removing his T-shirt and turning to face me. He put it over my head as if I were a child. He looked down and nodded, looking content to have me covered.

Jay snarled.

My gaze met his. "Jayson, it's okay. I promise. He doesn't feel like he'd hurt me."

"I don't give a shit what he feels like to you," snapped Jay. "His pack isn't known for playing well with others. Him showing up here, out of the blue, uninvited, is a big fucking red flag."

"Och, wolf, I've been trying to tell you that we're tracking a darkness that is indescribable. It is here, in your city, or do yer own men make a habit of trying to kill yer woman?" Shaw asked, keeping me close to him, as if he was worried another attempt would be made on me. "They are under the influence of the darkness. They will have no memory of attacking yer woman. I've seen this play out time and time again. Trust me when I say, if we do nae find a way to stop it, it can and *will* take yer woman from you, and leave you a shell of a man."

I thought about what he was saying. "You're here chasing Reynaud?" I asked.

Shaw nodded. "He's nae easy to track."

I groaned and rubbed the spot on my neck where he'd bitten me. "Seems hard to shake. Then there is the whole bit with the tall, great-looking, full of himself…oh, and he can mind-jack people against their will. Real sweet guy. Can't wait to spend more time with him."

A panicked look came over Shaw. "Stay away from him. As far as you can. He hides behind a smile, but on the inside, he carries a darkness that is as old as time. A darkness that feeds off chaos. A darkness that can control almost any supernatural with ease. As you well know from what happened to you several nights back."

"How the hell do you know what happened to her?" demanded Jay.

"I was there. My men and I interrupted what could have ended verra poorly."

I closed my eyes for a moment. "I'm trying to stay away from him, but he keeps invading my dreams. He did it tonight, right before the wolves turned on me."

Jay gasped. "Baby, I'm sorry I left you alone.

Sam came for me, to tell me Shaw and his men had shown up, and I didn't want to wake you. I should have stayed with you. I'm so fucking sorry. And I'm sorry my own men turned on you."

Shaw looked at him. "There is nothing you could have done to stop it from happening. There is a guid chance he'd have used you to try to harm her, had you been closer to her."

Jay came towards me and tried to hug me.

I moved closer to Shaw.

Jay stopped. "Baby, what did you dream about?"

I sighed. "I thought I was awake," I admitted. "I thought you were behind me in bed, holding me, but you were colder than you normally are."

Jay stiffened. "And?"

"And then I looked at the foot of the bed, and you were there. That didn't make any sense. How could you be in two places at once? Then I felt Reynaud's darkness blanketing me and the area. It was him in the bed with me, Jay. And he was doing something to you, making your wolf come up. Then you attacked me."

Wiping his hands over his face, he looked as

if he was about to be sick. "Christ, baby. No. I wouldn't hurt you. Ever. I love you."

I froze. "Uh, Jay?"

He swept his gaze over me. "Baby, I love you. Get over it."

Shaw put an arm around me and gave me a sideways squeeze. "Lass, yer pale."

I glanced up at him.

Shaw snickered. "Gonzales, the rumor mill had you being far better with the ladies than this."

I grunted. "He thinks we're mates."

"And you?" asked Shaw. "What do you think, lass?"

My gaze flickered to Jay, who was fighting the urge to come to me and, if I was right, still considering attacking Shaw for touching me. My mind raced with everything Jay and I had been through since meeting. And how the last six months had turned our worlds upside down. My bottom lip trembled as I spoke. "I think I might be falling in love with him too, but I'm scared to let him have that much power over me. I'm afraid he'll turn out to be like the other two men in my life who meant everything to me. That he'll break my heart."

Jay put his arms out, letting me come to him.

I did.

He picked me up and hugged me tightly, whispering softly in my ear, "I love you so fucking much, baby. Never doubt that. I'm not walking out on you—ever. I'm not Sam. I'm not your father. I'm here for the long haul. You want me gone, you're going to have to kill me. That's the only way you're getting rid of me."

I put my head against his chest for a second before I realized all the men in the place had heard him whispering to me. Cringing, I pushed to get down. "Jay, we have an audience."

"Good," he said, setting me on my feet but keeping me close. He looked out at the gathered crowd. "I know that only a portion of the pack is here, and I'd wanted to announce this in front of everyone at once, but what happened here tonight has made it clear the word needs to be spread now. She is my mate. To harm her is to harm me."

Whispers filled the room.

"You haven't claimed her," someone said from the back of the room. "We'd smell your mark on her if you had."

He stared out at the crowd. "Should you ever find yourself in a position where your mate is a slayer, you'll learn quickly that if you make any sudden moves, you're begging for an ass-kicking. And claiming her before she's fully wrapped her mind around the fact she's my mate would be a very sudden move. And I like my ass not kicked."

The men laughed.

Samuel entered from outside.

"The wolf from the pool?" I asked, worried about him.

"He's fine, but still in shifted form. I had men take him down to a holding cell," said Samuel. "Jay, he's not listening to reason. Whatever is pulling his strings is powerful."

Jay kissed the top of my head. "Why would Reynaud use my men to hurt you when it's very clear he wants to keep you for himself, not kill you?"

Shaw sighed. "He wants yer woman in a carnal way. It's a game to him. He can test her skills and still gain her for himself."

I tensed.

Shaw glanced back at his men before staring at Jay. "He'll nae stop coming for her.

When he gets fixated on a female, he stops at nothing to have them, and when it becomes clear they will nae bend to his whims, ever, he'll have someone close to you, someone you trust—maybe even you, yerself—slaughter her."

A low grumble came from Jay.

I pressed my hand to his chest. "Jayson, stop. Losing control won't fix this. I could lead him away from here. Take him somewhere he can't do so much damage."

Jay roared, "Like fucking hell! You are not to be near him!"

Romeo moved closer to us quickly, touching Jay's shoulder. "Easy there. And no, you can't lock her away for her own safety. She'll geld you, and you know it."

Jay was thinking of locking me away?

Shaw reached a hand out to Jay. "Can we set aside pack rules and find a way to stop this bastard before he kills your woman as he did mine?"

I faced him. "He killed your mate?"

Shaw swallowed hard. "She was nae my true mate, but I loved her greatly, and we had a family. Reynaud ruined all of that. He stole it from me, and I've nae stopped tracking him since."

I rubbed Jay's chest. "We have to stop him. We should pull together everyone. Zachariah can get the vampire dens that are trustworthy in the city to stand with us. I can call Exavier and have him reach out to the Faes here. Anyone else we can figure out as well. Maybe if we all stand together, we can take him down."

Jay glanced at his pack. "From what I'm sure you've all realized, we've got a problem. The club I've tasked many of you with watching is owned and operated by a vampire named Reynaud. He's got a hell of a lot of power. Enough to control some of you without issue, as you saw tonight. I've never stood against anything like him, and I can't ask any of you to do so. I'll understand if you want to walk away now and not join in this fight."

A man with shoulder-length blond hair stepped out from the crowd. He focused on Shaw. "He really do what you said to your family?"

Shaw nodded. "Aye. He wanted my wife. He stalked her at first, and when he realized she wasnae going to walk out on our child and me,

Reynaud decided he would make sure no one could have her."

Two of Shaw's men stepped closer to him, each putting a hand on his shoulder as they stood to his sides. Both were familiar to me, as was Shaw, yet I couldn't place any of them.

"It was just over twenty years since it all happened," admitted Shaw. "There's nae a day that goes by that I don't think of her and my wee ones."

"He killed your family?" asked another of Jay's pack members.

Shaw stiffened. "Aye, he destroyed my family."

My heart broke for the man, his voice was full of emotions that I'm sure an alpha male wasn't big on sharing with groups.

The blond who asked Shaw a question looked to Jay. "Is the redhead your true mate?"

"Yes," answered Jay.

"And this sick fuck fanger wants her for himself?" the man questioned.

Jay nodded.

"I'm in on hunting him," said the man.

Jay's pack members began stepping forward,

one by one, all committing to the cause. Not one walked away.

I couldn't help but tear up at the sight of the devotion and loyalty they had to Jay. They didn't just respect him, they loved him. Like a giant family. He was right, being with him meant you got all of this—the entire family.

Jay eased around me and went to Shaw. He drew Shaw into a manly embrace. "You have my help and that of my pack. I'll send word to the rest of them, giving them a choice to join or sit this out."

Shaw patted Jay's back and stepped back, nodding.

21

JAY STARED AROUND HIS BEDROOM AND TOOK A deep breath.

I cringed. "Sorry about your room. I swear I tried to minimize the damage to it, and to your men."

His brown gaze found me. "Gina, I don't give a shit about the room. I can't stop thinking about how I left you alone, in *our* room, and my own people hurt you."

Jay made his way to the open French doors. He looked down from the balcony before putting his palms to the banister and lowering his head. "You fell from here and hit the pool?"

He looked as if he was going to be sick.

"Again, spoiler alert, I lived."

He groaned. "I hate that my men did it."

I stayed near the entrance to the room. "You can't blame your guys. They're victims of this too."

He faced me. "That sick fuck took our space, our sanctuary, and turned it into this."

I stiffened. "I'm sorry. I didn't mean to bring this down on you and your men. I can go."

He stalked across the room to me. "Baby, you do understand that when I say *our* sanctuary, I mean you and me. I know you've not wrapped your mind around who I am to you, but, Gina, you're my mate. This is your home too. *Our* home."

I wasn't sure how to respond. My mind was a jumbled mess. "I'd like to take a shower."

He nodded and then glanced at the bed. "He made me turn on you...in the dream?"

"Yes."

"And I hurt you?"

I nodded.

Jay paled. "How the hell is he even getting into your dreams, let alone able to influence my men from a distance?"

"I don't know, but he is."

He faced the French doors. "Gina, I know you don't believe I'm your mate. That you think my wires are crossed. They're not. And deep down, I know if I don't claim you, that fucking vampire is going to win. That in the end, he'll rip you away from me."

Opening my mouth, I intended to protest, but stopped, choosing instead to sit on the edge of the bed. Jay had respected my request for him to hold off on claiming me. It seemed like a stupid request now. Not to mention, I shared Jay's fear, though it wasn't for myself. It was for him.

If he didn't claim me, Reynaud would hurt him. I just knew it.

Much to my surprise, my epiphany didn't make me sick to my stomach. The idea of the man I was clearly in love with being hurt was what made me want to puke.

I stood. "Jayson."

He looked at me, his entire body stiff and rigid.

"You're right."

He actually glanced behind him, as if I might not be talking to him. "Gina?"

I grunted. "Yeah, live it up. Those words won't be said much in our marriage—at least not from me. I'm sure you'll be saying them often."

A tic started in his jaw. "What are you saying? Be very clear. No jokes. No sarcasm."

"Seeing Reynaud use you in my dream, and just how much power and reach he has in his waking hours, freaked me out. The thought of you being hurt or controlled by him somehow… I can't even wrap my mind around it." I walked to him slowly. "Thank you for going out of your way to honor my request that you give us time to get to know each other on a sexual level before you give in to your wolf."

He glanced away.

"But, Jay, you and your wolf are right. I'm not willing to risk your life in order to keep denying what I get now is true. I can't promise the road with me will be smooth and without its bumps, but I *can* tell you I want to make the journey with you," I said, my voice low.

"Gina, say it," he said, his voice deep.

"You're right. We're mates. And I shouldn't have asked you to avoid claiming me when it felt right to you." I bit my lower lip, greatly disliking being put on the spot. I'd hoped he'd just grab me, fuck me, bite me and call it a win.

Trust Jay to pick that moment to control his libido.

"Jayson, if you still want me, I'm yours."

He touched my cheek. "Are you telling me I can claim you? That you understand it will make you my wife, and me your—"

Grumbling, I nodded. "Yes, but if you think 'honor and obey' is going to come into our marriage, you are dead wrong. I'll kick your ass if you pull that crap on me."

His lips twitched. "Baby, I like everything I have attached to me. But you need to understand that protecting you is and will be my number one priority, and sometimes that will leave me coming off as controlling. Know that I'm not trying to be. And do your best to avoid blowing my cousin when you're pissed at me."

Laughter bubbled up and out of me. "I'd rather just obey."

He snorted. "I swear you live to butt heads with me."

"Someone has to. Or you'd be here in your ivory tower, losing touch with reality," I said with a wink.

He drew me closer to him. "Gina, if we start this, I'm not going to be able to pull back like I did before—not with knowing how much danger you're in. You're either in all the way, or we don't start the claiming yet and take our chances with Reynaud."

"I'm all in," I said.

He had me undressed in seconds, following suit.

He lifted me and took me to the bed, crawling up and over it, carrying me as he did. When he lay down, I was pinned under him. Jay slid up even faster and lined up with my core before driving home.

I cried out, clawing him, drawing blood as I did.

He wasn't slow, and he wasn't gentle, but he was what I needed him to be.

Alpha.

Pounding into me, he held me to him, drilling me into the bed. He was going to break me in two in the best way possible.

I was sure of it.

My lower half began to numb, and my toes curled. My inner thighs tingled, and I scratched him open more. I hit my zenith and orgasmed so hard that my pussy seized hold of his cock, making him moan, and me cry out.

Jay's jaw went slack. He increased his pace and went balls deep.

I cried out from the bite of pain and the mix of pleasure.

He growled. "Mine."

Something in me clicked. "Not yet, Jay! Hold it. Just a bit longer."

The sensation of a thousand bees buzzing around me kicked into high gear. It felt as if the temperature in the room dropped as well. Something built deep within me, and fear for Jay consumed me.

I pushed at him, but he didn't budge. "Off! Go! Jay!"

He grunted and kept fucking me.

I cried out—and something burst free from me. It felt like a charge of static. It went right at Jay, hitting him, going through him, making him cry out as well. I opened my mouth to scream, terrified I'd somehow hurt him, but what came out stunned me to my core.

"Do it now, Jay, take me and make me yours *now*, while my claim is riding hide in you!" I said, the static energy growing between us. "My side is done. Complete your half now!"

He caught my wrists and jerked my hands

above my head, his cock ramming into me
again. He pummeled my body in the best way
possible. I felt every movement, each one
drawing moans from me.

Jay was like a piston, and I fought for air in
between gasps of pleasure. I managed to release
my wrists and grabbed tight to him as the
strange static energy in the air pulsed back and
forth from me to him, over and over again.

Jay locked gazes with me. "Mine!"

I yanked on him, wanting his head down on
my shoulder. I was like a possessed woman. My
hands had a mind of their own, pulling on him.
He dipped his head, and the slightest of pains
washed through my shoulder before pleasure
like I'd never known consumed me fully.

My body burst, and for a moment, I saw
nothing but a pulse of white. Instantly it felt as
if I was connected to Jay by a rope. I climaxed
again and shouted out, holding his head to me,
knowing he was biting me and sealing the deal.

My body tingled more, and the aches and
pains I'd had from falling over the balcony and
my scrape with the wolves eased.

Jay released my shoulder and licked the spot
where he'd bitten me. He slammed into me as I

hit culmination again, my entire body burning with pleasure. His cock twitched, and I knew he was coming.

I kissed the side of his face, keeping my legs wrapped around his waist.

His lips found mine, and he kept moving, slowly now inside of me, as he kissed me tenderly. When he broke the kiss, he stared down at me and grinned, dimples forming on both cheeks. "Gina, I swear to you, I'll be the best damned husband ever."

I knew he would be, but our relationship had always been founded on an odd sense of humor. I clucked my tongue on the inside of my cheek. "You better, or I'm going to blow——"

He laughed and kissed me again.

I touched his cheeks. "Hon, we should shower. I smell like the pool and wet dogs."

"Mmm, you smell perfect."

I groaned.

22

FRESHLY SHOWERED AND WEARING YOGA PANTS and a fitted T-shirt that Jay just *happened* to have in my size, I sat on a stool at the long center island in his kitchen. My damp hair was drawn into a ponytail. I sipped the tea one of the men had made and stared at my bandaged hand. It hadn't needed dressed but Jay had insisted. I humored him.

Jay was practically plastered to me as he stood there, his hands on my shoulders. He'd not stopped touching me since he claimed me. He'd refused to allow me to shower alone. He'd stood there, leaning against the wall in the bathroom, watching the door as if Reynaud would come bursting in at any second.

Jay looked at the end of the island in the

kitchen and took a deep breath. "Tell me every-thing you know about this vampire."

Shaw and the two men who had come into the kitchen with him shared a look. "The vampire was my wife's true mate."

I stiffened, feeling bad for the guy's wife.

Shaw sipped his coffee. "The first time I met her, she nearly killed me."

I lifted a brow. That didn't sound like the best way to start a relationship. Though, I'd had worse dates.

The smallest of smiles touched Shaw's lips, and he ran his hand through his long beard. "She was a natural-born slayer, and I'd been chasing a were-coyote down a back alley. I leaped over a huge dumpster, and this tiny woman knocked me on my arse and held a knife to my chest, demanding to know what I was doing there."

The men with Shaw laughed softly.

Jay kissed the top of my head as he continued to rub my shoulders. "How could you claim her if she was a natural-born slayer? I ran into that with Gina and needed some help from higher-ups."

"Used my magik," responded Shaw. "I'm

nae proud that I basically tricked nature, but I wanted her and she me."

Shaw paused his storytelling. His attention went to Jay, and he tipped his head in a way that screamed badass.

The next thing I knew, Romeo and Samuel were moving to each side of me, and Shaw's men closed ranks around him. He growled. "Yer verra touchy-feely with her. And am I smelling a claim on her?"

Jay kept touching me. "You are, McKay. Though, I have to admit, I'm sort of shocked she let me do it. I figured she'd rip my nuts off before she even considered agreeing to be my wife. She might be the most stubborn woman I've ever met."

Shaw's eyes crinkled with mirth and the tension in him lessened. "Aye. My wife was much the same way. She too was a redhead. She told me no more than once too when I asked for her hand in marriage. Eventually, I wore her down. Dinnae dampen her temper any though."

His men smiled.

"I remember how much you got on her nerves to start with, Shaw," said the brown-haired man next to him. "She thought you were a smooth-talking ladies' man who boned anything that moved."

I couldn't help but look up at Jay where he stood behind me.

He cringed and rubbed my shoulders more. "Baby, I've explained to you. That's in the past."

"Uh-huh," I murmured. "It'd better be, or I'll rip pieces of you off."

The men in the kitchen grinned at Jay as if they thought me threatening his manhood was humorous. I'm not sure they understood I would and could follow through on it all.

"I recall my wife saying much the same thing to me. Och, she wouldnae listen as I tried to tell her that I'd nae look at another if she gave me a chance," said Shaw, staring at the window in the kitchen as if deep in thought. "Took me a year to talk her into it. In that year, I watched over her from a safe distance, worried she'd be hurt in her line of work. I'd track the things that did her harm, and I'd make their deaths painful."

Wow. The guy was basically the Scottish version of Jay. I refrained from saying as much mainly because it was freaking me out, but I was sure why.

Jay bent and kissed my cheek as if he'd read my mind.

"Over the year I followed my wife around, shadowing her, I saw how paranoid she was. How she never let her guard down," he said, sighing. "It's an occupational hazard to a degree, but she far exceeded normal levels of fear. One night, she confessed that she knew her mate. That she'd met him and that he was a monster. That he was a vampire who had done something—made a deal with darkness ages ago. It changed him enough that she was able to have feelings for me, and me her."

The brown-haired man touched Shaw's arm. "You loved her. She knew that."

"Aye. It dinnae matter that she wasnae my true mate. I carry enough magik in me to over-ride nature to a degree. I wed her in a church and before long, we had a wee one on the way," he said, looking down at his coffee cup. "My wife wasnae excited to start. I dinnae understand why. I learned later that she'd begun to dream of her true mate again—Reynaud. In the dreams, he taunted her and threatened her. He threatened me and the unborn babe as well."

My hand moved up and over Jay's as I

thought about the dream I'd had. He'd not been the man I knew and had deep feelings for. He'd been a stranger to me in the dream. A deadly man that I no longer knew.

Jay bear-hugged me. "Baby, I'd never hurt you. Know that."

Shaw watched Jay as if prepared to strike. "You do nae have to keep touching her that much. It makes me uncomfortable and I find myself wanting to harm you greatly."

"Ballsy considering you're in my house," reminded Jay.

Shaw shrugged. "Does nae change the way of it, Gonzales."

Samuel snorted. "Wow. You're getting cock blocked by a guy who just got here. Not that I'm complaining or anything."

A growl sounded from Jay and he eased his hold on me. I stood quickly, putting myself between Samuel and Jay. I touched each of their chests. "Boys. Play nice. I've had a really crappy week. Can we maybe not argue?"

Samuel's jaw set. "Yes."

Romeo touched my arm. "You understand there is only so much Jay can tolerate from Samuel, right? It's kind of a pack thing."

I stepped in close to Jay. "I know. They're cousins. They don't need to fight. And let's be honest, I'm not really worth arguing over."

Shaw stood fast. "Do nae let me hear you talk of yerself that way again. You are worth everything. And if they do nae stop, I will handle both of them."

"Shaw, take it easy," said the blond with him. "This isn't like you. What Jay and his woman do is their business. Not ours. Not yours. You're acting like you've got a stake in this. You don't, man."

"Christian, I will nae take it easy. The lass thinks she's unworthy of attention." The way Shaw watched me, with emotions laid bare for all to see, was both unnerving and comforting.

I wasn't sure why.

For a second, I could have sworn I felt his pain, his deep longing for something. It wasn't sexual in any way. It was protective and nurturing. It also left me walking around Jay and taking the stool near Shaw.

My hand went to the man's. "Thank you for what you said."

I worried Jay would alpha out over me touching the man. He didn't. He did narrow his gaze on us as he watched the scene unfolding.

Shaw took my hand in his and squeezed gently. "I have the sense you werenae told of yer worth enough. That you see yerself as disposable to others."

Romeo cleared his throat. "She does. I think she lives life waiting for the other shoe to drop. Scared that yet another man she cares for will just walk out of her life. It's what they've all done to her in the past."

Samuel averted his gaze. He quickly busied himself by making a cup of coffee.

Jay stood stoic, no anger radiating from him whatsoever. Which surprised me, since he seemed to have great issues with me being near other men.

My attention went to Romeo. The urge to throttle him for sharing my emotions didn't come. I had to wonder if being married to Jay was starting to mellow me out.

I shuddered.

Shaw took his hand from mine and touched my chin, turning my face to his. "Lass, yer nae disposable."

Christian exhaled, long and slow. "Shaw, you're going to freak the poor girl out."

I grabbed Shaw's hand and shook my head. "No. You don't scare me."

"Guid," he said, standing and taking my head in his hands. He then kissed the top of my head. "You never have to fear me, lass. I'll allow no harm to come to you again."

A nervous laugh escaped me. "Thanks, but you don't need to worry about me. I get by just fine on my own."

Jay crossed his arms over his chest, his chocolate gaze fixed on me. "You're not alone, baby. You have me. You have the pack."

Romeo grinned. "She's apparently got Shaw as well. Interesting."

I quirked a brow. "Oracle, you and I are gonna have a come-to-Jesus moment soon."

Laughing, Romeo lifted his cup of coffee. "I'm sure of it."

Shaw draped an arm over my shoulder. "Gonzales, you have a treasure here. Cherish her, or you will have me to deal with."

I couldn't help but laugh softly.

Romeo's gaze slid to Shaw. "Very fatherly of you."

Shaw squeezed me gently. "I have a soft spot for the lass. Get over it."

Christian sighed. "Shaw."

I looked up at Shaw. "Did your wife find a way to stop the dreams about Reynaud?"

He shook his head as sadness filled his gaze. "She lived in fear of him coming for her again. Her worry was for our babe and for me. When our daughter came, she was the joy of our lives. Such a gift."

For a second, I thought the man would squeeze me until my head popped clean off.

He loosened his grip on me some. "Things were guid for my family for two years before it all changed. My wee one would wake, screaming from her sleep, leaping at me and clinging to me, shaking nonstop. The night terrors were so bad that I would sit in her room and hold her in a rocking chair while she slept," he said softly, his arm still around me. "One night, I sensed *it* there, lingering near her toddler bed, near her."

The brown-haired guy swallowed hard. "She was so tiny and so scared. Christian and I were powerless to protect her from it all."

"Mason, I know you did all you could," said

Shaw. "I remember you there, in the doorway of her room, ready to step in and assist should the need arise."

"She was just a baby then. Barely two years old, and that monster was terrorizing her from afar," Mason said, looking at the counter. "I could feel it, but I couldn't see it."

Shaw continued. "Pure evil was there, hovering over my babe. It was then I knew the night terrors she suffered were from *him*. When my wife burst into the bedroom one night and told us what she'd learned in one of the dreams that bastard caused, I almost threw up on the spot."

I looked up at Shaw. "What did she find out?"

His jaw tightened. "She told me her mate had not only found her location again, but confirmed he'd learned of our daughter. Learned that my wife had not only betrayed him by taking another to her bed, but a child had come of the union. And that the child could be a match for him one day—or close enough to one that he could use his magik to make it so. As I'd done with his mate, he planned to do to my daughter."

I cringed for him. If I had a daughter, I'd never want Reynaud around her.

"I'd never met the man, and I dinnae think he was that big of a threat. I thought my wife was overreacting. I cast protection spells over the wee one so her sleep could nae be interfered with by outside sources and continued to sit with her at night, just in case. By that point, she was so scared of sleeping that she fought it with all she had."

Mason smiled a bit. "She was obstinate. Like you, Shaw. How many times did you have to sing her to sleep?"

My chest tightened as I thought of my father singing to me. Just thinking about it filled me with warmth.

"I should have listened to my wife and her warnings. I thought everything was fine. That the danger was no more," Shaw whispered. "I even used my gifts to assure my wife carried another child. She'd been against it at first, but I swayed her thoughts on the matter. She had warned me that Reynaud had shown her in dreams that he would use those she cared for against her. I dinnae think that possible."

I stiffened, and Jay perked, his attention locked on Shaw. "Did he?"

"Aye. I believed myself all powerful. That as alpha, I could handle anything and that no vampire would ever dream to harm my family, that they'd nae want the force of the pack against them," said Shaw before sipping his coffee again, his other arm going over my shoulders as he stood next to me. "He is able to bend the will of some. Not all, but enough. He bent the will of a man I trusted fully. My daughter's godfather. He was to be watching over my wife and wee one while I tended to pack matters. In the end, I found him sobbing outside of my house, staring at his hands that were covered in blood, trying desperately to figure out why he'd done what he'd done. And when I entered my home, I saw the devastation Reynaud is capable of."

He closed his eyes and tears dripped freely down his cheeks. "My ego and arrogance cost me my wife and unborn babe. And in the end, I lost my daughter as well."

I twisted on the stool and slid my arms around his waist, hugging him and putting my cheek on his chest.

He squeezed me gently and sighed. "Reynaud went to ground for years and only recently resurfaced. I believe Reynaud is hunting for the one he sees as a possible mate. We're here to try to put a stop to him before he can do any more harm."

I couldn't stand seeing him cry.

"You said he saw your daughter as a possible match," said Jay, his gaze sliding to me.

"Aye."

Jay stiffened. "Shaw, does Reynaud have access to your daughter now?"

"No. Well, I do nae think so," said Shaw, his voice barely there. "We've nae had contact in a while. It was for the best. Though, it killed me inside. I had to make the hardest decision of my long life."

Christian swallowed hard. "It wasn't one you made lightly."

"No, it wasn't," added Mason. "And we were all there with you. We made a choice together, as pack, as family."

"You did what had to be done, Shaw," said Christian. "Even though it killed a piece of you to do what you did."

I released my hold on him. "What did you do?"

Shaw's tears came faster. "I assured she'd be far from me, and that I'd nae know where she was or who she was with. I dinnae want to risk Reynaud somehow reading my thoughts and finding her through me."

I tensed as emotions from my past surfaced. My father had done the same thing and it hurt me to hear about another repeating that mistake. "You gave your daughter away?"

"Aye," he said, choking back a sob.

Hurt that he'd do something like that, I moved off the stool quickly and found Jay there, sweeping me into his arms. He held me to him and rocked me in place.

"Lass?" asked Shaw.

I couldn't even look at the man. I knew what it was like to be on the other side of that. To have a father hand me to strangers and banish from my life. It wasn't fun.

23

"Jayson," said one of Jay's men as he came rushing into the kitchen. "We've got nearly every wolf affected by the vampire back to themselves except one. He's demanding to talk to you and your mate. But, Jay...it doesn't sound like Jesse. When he talks, there's a heavy French accent. He's from Texas."

Everyone in the kitchen hurried to follow the man as he raced through Jay's massive home. Right before we were about to head through a large door, Jay spun and grabbed me. He looked to Shaw. "Keep her far from him."

My expression was murderous. "He's doing this to your man because of me! I'm going in."

Shaw braced himself. "Lass, remain here

with Christian and Mason. Gonzales and I will enter the web Reynaud weaves."

Seeing that I wasn't going to talk the two alphas out of anything, I nodded, letting them believe I'd listen. One would think Jay would be smart enough to realize my compliance meant I wasn't going to obey.

He ran through the door and down a large set of steps. Once they were through the door and gone a good five minutes, I glanced at Christian and Mason. "I'm going too. Want to end up hurt trying to stop me, or do you want to see if we can all finally find a way to stop this dickwad?"

They shared a look and sighed.

"I'll lead, you follow," said Mason.

I shrugged. "Works for me."

We emerged from the staircase area into a huge basement. There were cells along one side, and I had to wonder what the hell Jay needed with a holding chamber under his house. I'd have questioned it more but shouting from the end of the hall demanded my attention.

I followed Mason as he ran down the hall with Christian close on my heels.

We found Jay and Shaw there, pacing in

front of a cell as a man with dark hair stood perfectly still within it. Romeo watched Jay and Shaw as if they might end up being the real problem.

He was probably right.

"Bring the slayer to me," said the man, sounding almost identical to Reynaud. "I sent you a message already, wolf. Did you not get it? I sent it through her—that I can reach her and your men at any moment, and with but a thought I can rip her away from you."

"You fucking touch her and I'll—" Jay clenched his fists as alpha poured off him.

"Bring her to me now!" Jesse, or whatever was controlling Jesse, demanded.

I pushed past Mason and Jay grabbed for me, yanking me back from the cell bars.

At the sight of me, a slow smile slid across Jesse's face. It was the same smile Reynaud used on me before. "Little slayer, good of you to join us."

I stepped out of Jay's hold. "What do you want, Reynaud?"

"So young and so bold," he said, unblinking and unmoving. It was as if Jesse were a marionette, not a real man.

"Is Jesse hurting with you controlling him?" I may not have known Jesse personally, but no one deserved to be body-jacked. Let alone body-jacked by an ancient blowhard.

He rotated his head in a slow manner. "No. Not yet. But know I can make him snap his own neck if I so choose."

My hands went to the cell bars. "Don't. You have nothing to prove. I know you're powerful. And they saw what you did with the wolves here. This isn't necessary."

"But it is amusing," he returned.

I curled my hands around the bars. "Why haven't you taken over *me*? Or Jay—beyond my dream? Even Romeo. Why Jesse? He doesn't know me. I don't know him."

Something flickered in his eyes, telling me he couldn't.

"You showed me in my dream that you could make Jay hurt me." I leaned in against the bars more. "Do it. Make Jay hurt me."

"What?" Jay shouted, while he grabbed me back from the cell. "Are you insane? Don't taunt him so he makes me hurt you."

Shaw came to my aid, standing by my side,

folding his arms over his chest. "Aye, make Jay harm her. Make *me* do it, even."

In the next second, Jesse grabbed his own head—and something deep inside me broke free.

One second, Jesse was there in the center of the cell, preparing to snap his own neck, and the next, he was flung against the back of the cell. His hands and legs were pinned out against the wall.

Reynaud looked to Shaw. "Interesting, you were unable to do this to me before."

Shaw looked at Jay, and then Christian and Mason. "It was nae my doing."

"Romeo?" asked Jay.

"Not me either, boss," said Romeo, sounding stunned.

Reynaud stared at me from Jesse's eyes. "This is a twist I did not see coming. Your mother was unable to wield magik. Her gifts only extended to slayer abilities, and while she was very skilled, she paled in comparison to you. I watched you kill over twenty of my men—and they were not low-level vampires. You took them out in mere minutes…with a pair of high heels, of all things."

I nearly laughed at him. "You knew my mother? Right."

"I did," he returned, still not blinking. "She was stunning. And the feel of being inside her was like nothing I've ever felt before. Though, I could have done without her screams. That did taint the moment."

I took a deep breath, refusing to let the sick bastard get under my skin. He didn't know my mother, he just wanted me riled so I'd stop asking him questions he didn't want to answer. I'd seen many bad guys try something similar. Though, none had claimed to know my mother before.

"You are taller than she was. Not by much, but enough," he said, looking anything but human with his unnatural stillness. "Your breasts are bigger as well. More to hold on to."

Jay and Shaw growled.

Reynaud liked the response he evoked in them.

I glanced at Romeo. "If Jay continues, remove him from the level. Christian, do the same with Shaw."

"I'm not fucking leaving," said Jay.

"Aye, neither am I, lass. And if he speaks of

yer…womanly parts again, I will crush him. I do nae care if he is in a fellow shifter."

I spun and glared at both Jay and Shaw. "Reynaud knows how to get you both going. He feeds off your anger and your hate. Stop playing into his hands."

Reynaud laughed. "So smart and so young. And so beautiful. As your mother was. I took no real joy in ending her life, but she left me no choice."

Something tugged at my gut that warned me he might not be lying as much as I thought he was.

"She did not heed my warnings. She did not surrender to me. I asked more than once nicely," he said, his gaze never wavering from me. "Even when I bent her will, she still would not remain with me. The moment I lifted my hold on her, she returned to her *lover*," he said, his gaze hardening as it slid to Shaw.

My temper began to rise, and with it came a clawing feeling in my gut. "To be clear, you had to use your vamp mojo on some woman you keep saying was my mother to get her to sleep with you? Reynaud, I thought you were better with the ladies than that. I mean, they all seemed taken with you at your club. Did you have to force yourself on her because she got to know the real you? The one who made some sort of deal with darkness?"

"Little slayer, I sense you doubt of the truth of my words. I have no reason to lie to you," he said softly. "And I had to bend her will because she took a lover and had the nerve to have a child with him—they went against nature. Against destiny…to have *you*. I nearly had her killed when I learned the truth. You were in her womb. Something told me to wait. That perhaps killing her before you arrived was unwise."

The urge to throttle him was great. But hitting him would only hurt Jesse, not Reynaud. "Should I thank you for being insane and obsessed with a woman who clearly didn't want you? Do you do this a lot? I mean, Shaw told us what you did to *his* wife. Make a habit of stalking women and killing them? No wonder you can't get any to commit. You're insane and sick."

He licked his lips. "I permitted her to birth you. I even allowed her to raise you for a few years. I thought perhaps she would see the light and realize the error of her ways. When she came back to me, I thought it was for good. But she only wanted to borrow power from me to have another child with her lover. He didn't know she'd come to barter with me."

I stiffened. "You made her be with you on her own, without influencing her, didn't you?"

"How can one force what is meant to be?" he asked, grinning like he was the Joker staring down Batman. "And she left with more than my power."

I drew back slightly.

Reynaud focused on Shaw. "She left my bed carrying *my* child. She was to end things with her lover. Her fake husband. She did not obey. And my child growing within her made her resistant to my influence. I would not permit a dirty animal to raise my child. And my mate's betrayal could go unpunished no longer."

I stiffened.

His gaze moved slowly to Shaw before returning to me. "Tell me, *Regina*, do you still remember her screams when your father's best friend ripped her apart in front of your very eyes? I remember them—as I was the one controlling the man who tore her to pieces. She died believing you were next. And you would have been, had the man I held in my power not had great love for you. He pushed me out, but not before my mate was dead. Consider this tale a cautionary one. Leave your wolf and return to me, or I will have him kill you…or I could simply force your father to do it, now that he's in your life once more."

Slowly, I turned to look at Shaw and really saw him. The tightness in my stomach grew as I tried to picture him without the full beard and long hair.

Shaw, Mason, and Christian gasped so loudly that I half expected Reynaud himself had popped up behind us in the large hall.

In a flash, Shaw was there, practically throwing me into Jay. He put himself in front of me, blocking my view of Jesse—or the thing currently pulling Jesse's strings. "I'll nae let you harm my daughter! I will be yer end!"

"You can no more protect your daughter than you could protect *my* mate," said Reynaud with a laugh. "Sleep tight, Gina. And keep an eye on your wolf. You never know when that temper of his will get the best of him."

Jay's hold on me bordered on painful, yet

the pain slid away, and a strange numbness came over me. It took a minute for my brain to fully connect what Reynaud had said. Shock made it hard for me to think clearly.

Shaw spun and ripped me from Jay's arms. He moved me to the end of the hall, near the staircase, and then cupped my face, his green gaze filled with moisture. "Regina? How did I nae see it? How did I nae know? You do nae carry my scent as you once did. How? You were just a wee one when I last saw you. Yer a young woman now. All grown. I should have seen through that. I should have known it was you. Baby girl, I'm so sorry."

I just stood there, my arms at my side, my entire body still numb as my head struggled with all I'd heard. After what felt like hours, I met Shaw's green gaze, realizing then how it was identical to mine. My brows met. "You're my…?"

His tears came fast and hard as he nodded. "Aye, lass."

I looked at Jay, like he'd have all the answers.

His eyes were moist as well. "Fiery One, he's your father. At first, I didn't put it together. I couldn't understand why you'd run to *him*, a total stranger, in the pool house, instead of to me—your mate. And then his reaction when the lewd comments were made about you…it wasn't rational. Not to mention, he's been giving me a hard time about touching you."

Mason stepped closer to me. He was crying too. "Look at you, Regina. All grown up now."

Christian laughed through his tears. "I knew that stubborn streak was familiar. We spent a lot of years guarding you. We should have recognized it was you."

I blinked several times before looking up at Shaw. "You left me. You took me to a hospital, and you walked away."

He closed his eyes and tipped his head back. "Aye, and there has nae been a day that I have nae hated myself for that choice."

"Shaw, there was no choice," said Mason. "Reynaud would have found her much sooner than now if we'd have kept her around us."

"How did he find me at all?" I asked, my voice low.

Jay cursed under his breath. "Exavier."

I eyed him. "Exavier would never hand my location over to a madman."

"No, baby," said Jay. "I don't think for a

minute he handed Reynaud anything. I told you that six months ago, Exavier took it upon himself to talk to the higher-ups. He knew we were mates, and he knew my wolf side was screwed up because you're a slayer. He fixed that."

Romeo gasped. "And because she's not actually just a slayer, it sent up a flare, alerting anyone who was looking for her where she was."

Christian looked at Shaw. "Six months ago, you gathered the rest of the pack and told us we had to keep our ears to the ground. That you knew Reynaud was back and that he was hunting your daughter."

His daughter.

The thought left me an emotional washing machine, all my feelings swishing around together, going nowhere, yet jumbled.

I backed out of Shaw's embrace, lowered my gaze and went for Jay.

Jay sighed. "Baby, don't shut him out. He did what he had to in order to keep you safe."

"He abandoned me, left me to be put into the system, and left me to figure out my gifts on my own." I sank against Jay. "I don't know that man anymore. Actually, I never really knew him at all, did I? Because the man I remember him being wouldn't have done that."

"Regina," Shaw said softly, his voice full of pain. "I do nae blame you for hating me. I hate myself. But I love you, baby girl. Know that. And the only way I could be sure Reynaud couldnae find you through me was to be sure *I* couldnae find you. I loved you enough to send you away. Knowing I'd never see you again."

24

I SAT ON JAY'S LIVING ROOM SOFA IN SOMETHING of a daze. So much had been dumped on me in such a short period of time that my brain had basically checked out and was not taking reservations for any more thoughts.

Romeo was next to me with a pint of rocky road ice cream at the ready. He seemed to think finding your long-lost father while in the middle of dealing with a nut-job master vampire warranted ice cream. We were way past ice cream at this point.

Way, way past.

Jay had tried to sit with me, but the constant hugging thing had grated on my nerves by minute four.

Shaw, or Dad, or whatever I was supposed

to call him now, had made an attempt to stay close to me.

It wasn't long before Romeo chased them both off and sat with me. He'd not said a word, which was perfect.

I ran my hands over my face and shook my head.

Romeo held out the ice cream for me.

This time I took it.

He produced a spoon without me having to ask.

I dug in and tried to offer him some as well.

He groaned. "Chocolate and wolves don't mix very well."

"Huh, never really thought of that before," I said, taking a big spoonful. "Why do you guys have it around?"

"Jay knows you like it," he said, as if that explained it all.

I ate more and then glanced at him. "My week has been super weird."

He grinned. "I'd say so. How are you doing with everything?"

"My dad is Scottish," I said, as if that was the biggest revelation I'd had as of late.

"I noticed." He nudged me lightly with his shoulder. "Explains your temper though."

I ate more ice cream. "Are they talking about me?"

Romeo was quiet a moment and I knew he was listening in on the conversation happening in the kitchen. He nodded. "Your father just threatened to neuter Jay for claiming you."

The ice cream was looking better and better. "Wait until he learns I was with Sam too."

Romeo smirked. "One alpha male sexual escapade revelation at a time."

I stilled. "He saved me when Reynaud first attacked me."

"Who? Sam?"

I shook my head. "My dad. He, Christian and Mason had been outside of the vampire club, watching it. Then when I got the flat tire and Reynaud came for me, my dad and the others showed up. I don't know what would have happened if they hadn't."

"Gina, he may not have recognized you as a grown woman, but deep down, he knew who you were to him on some level. He'd already gone rounds with the vampire in the past. He had to know confronting him like that wouldn't end well for him, but he did it anyway. He did it for you."

I leaned against him. "My mom was Reynaud's mate?"

"Sounds like it," Romeo returned in a hushed tone. "If I was her, I wouldn't have stayed with him either."

"I'd have slit his damn throat while he was sleeping," I added before eating more ice cream.

"Why did you push him to take over Jay and hurt you?" he asked. "I couldn't read you then. You shut down on me."

With a sigh, I handed him the ice cream. "My gut says he can't force Jay, but he wants me to think he can. He didn't use my dad against my mom."

Romeo tensed. "You think they're immune?"

"I think they're too strong for him to invade their minds. I think Reynaud's not as strong as he used to be, and even back then, he still couldn't use my dad for his evil bidding." I pushed the ice cream away more. "If I eat another bite, I'll be sick."

He was quiet a second before another man came in and took the ice cream.

"I wish I could mind talk to them all," I said with snort. "It would save so much time if I could read Jay's mind."

"He wears his emotions for you on his sleeve," returned Romeo. "He loves you so much, Gina. And he's going to be a great husband and father."

"Father?" I asked. "Uh, let's not go there just yet. I need some time before we cross that bridge. Like a century or so."

He eyed me but said nothing.

I remained pressed to him. "Jay is going to do something stupid and attack Reynaud full-on, isn't he? Like Zachariah said he would."

"Probably. Your dad seems onboard for it too. I think fear for you is driving them both," admitted Romeo. "And, Gina, you should know they won't have their heads on straight. Jay's mind is going a thousand miles per hour right now. His emotions are all over the place too."

"That's what I'm afraid of," I whispered. "They're all going to end up hurt or worse."

"More than likely," he said, and I appreciated his honesty.

"What are they talking about now?"

He licked his lower lip. "Their harebrained

plan to kill Reynaud. It's not going to work. They all know it too, but they can't think of anything else to do."

I thought back to the night at the club. The huge metal door with the guard on it kept popping into my head. My hand went to Romeo's knee. "Darkness like Reynaud has in him isn't normal, right?"

"I've never heard of it before."

"Do you think it comes from somewhere? Like maybe Reynaud is plugged in to it, like a power source, and where he goes, it has to travel with him? Or do you think it's always there inside of him?"

Romeo thought on it a bit. "I don't know. What makes you think it might not always be in him?"

"I felt it crawling over the club when I was there. Like it was vines coming from an evil plant." I clutched his knee. "Stupid thought. I know."

"Gina, the very fact you said it tells me it's not stupid at all. You come from a long line of slayers from the sounds of it, and you have magik and shifter in you. I'm inclined to trust your knee-jerk reactions."

The doorbell rang, and Romeo put an arm around me protectively.

I cast him an unamused look. "I doubt bad guys knock."

Two of Jay's men answered the door, and were suddenly shoved into the foyer.

"Where is she?" demanded Lindsay, sounding pissed.

I hurried in that direction just in time to find my best friend storming in, her hand on her stomach and a determined look on her face. Right behind her was my other closest friend —Myra.

Myra laughed as Lindsay charged in. "Dear Lord, woman. You were scary before pregnancy hormones were added. No wonder why Exavier is thinking of wearing a cup."

"Don't even say his name to me right now," snapped Lindsay. She spotted me and beamed, coming right for me. She yanked me to her and held me tight, like I was a rag doll. "We were worried about you!"

Myra helped to pry Lindsay off me and then she gave me a fast hug, knowing I wasn't a huge fan of them. "Look who I ran into out front."

I glanced past them both. "Where is Exavier?"

Lindsay huffed. "I left his ass at home."

"It would appear the baby has Daddy's ability to pop in and out of places," said Myra, looking as if she wanted to say more but thinking better of it.

"What are you both doing here?" I asked. "Myra, you were supposed to be with your mom longer."

They shared a look.

Myra grinned. "Sweets, there is no way we were leaving you alone with everything going on. Lindsay called me when the slayers went down. I caught the first flight back. No one messes with my friends."

Lindsay hugged me again. "And Jay texted to say you needed someone to talk to and that you wouldn't let him hug you anymore."

A laugh burst free from me. "So he sent for backup?"

She blinked back tears. "Gina, he also texted to say your birth father is here."

"Ooh, I missed that tidbit," said Myra. "Is he here, here? Or in the city?"

Romeo put his hands on my shoulders.

"*Here*, here. He's in the kitchen with Jay and the others, trying to formulate a plan to take down the new big baddie in town."

I looked at my friends. "Cutting to the end —it's not going to work."

Myra groaned. "Men. They're shit at planning."

"I hate all men," snapped Lindsay, eyeing Romeo.

He stiffened.

"Get her the rocky road," I said. "It's the only way to stay safe."

He hurried off.

Jay came rushing down the hall at us, his phone pressed to his ear. "Yes, Exavier, I'm looking at her right now. She looks pissed. What did you do? You told her she wasn't allowed to see Gina until all this blew over? Fuck, man, do you still have balls or did she cut them off?"

I smiled. "Might want to suggest the cup to him, Jay."

"Calm down. She's here in my house. Myra is with her. No. I'm not going to let her leave," said Jay, before licking his lips and looking at me. "I mean, Gina won't let her leave. I like my balls just where they are."

"I like them there too, hon," I said.

He growled in a sexy way.

Myra sniffed the air. "Holy shit! He did it. He claimed you!"

Lindsay squealed so loud that Myra and I actually jumped.

I touched my chest. "Linds! You almost gave me a heart attack."

"Gonzales, are you going to talk on the damn phone all night or are you going to help think of something to stop this son of a bitch?" asked Shaw as he came down the hall.

Myra and Lindsay smiled wide and leaned against one another.

Lindsay bit her lower lip. "Wow. Who's the hottie?"

I paled.

Myra stared at Shaw as if she were thinking of taking him for a test ride. "Sexy *and* Scottish."

I shot in front of them and put my arms out. "Stop mentally undressing my dad."

My friends drew back.

"Gina, your dad is *hot*! Like fifty-out-of-ten kind of hot," said Lindsay.

"You're mated to the Prince of Darkness, stop rating my dad. It's gross," I said sternly.

"Pregnancy makes me very, very horny," she blurted. "I can look but not touch. Can he take his shirt off?"

"What? No! Stop. He's not hot. He's…he's my *dad*!" I glanced back at him to find Shaw trying hard not to laugh. "It's not funny."

"'Tis a wee bit funny, lass," he said.

I couldn't help but laugh some before tearing up.

He pushed Jay out of the way and came to me, sweeping me up in his arms. He hugged me tight to him. "I'm sorry again for leaving you, lass."

"I know," I whispered, hugging him back. "But if you take your shirt off right now, I'm going to go back to being mad at you."

He laughed hard and set me down gently. He held me to him and faced Lindsay and Myra. "Yer friends of my daughter?"

They stared dreamily at him and nodded.

Now off the phone, Jay eased up alongside me. "Why in the hell do Lindsay and Myra look like that?"

I groaned. "They think my dad is hot."

Jay didn't bother to hide his laughter. "I think he's a dick, but he's growing on me slowly."

"Yer nae growing on me one bit, Gonzales," said my father sternly. "I do nae like that you claimed my daughter."

"She's my *mate*," said Jay, as if he'd said it a hundred times before to the man.

"Och, I do nae care. She's my babe. No man is guid enough for her," returned my father. "Nae you. Nae anyone."

I put my hand on my father's chest. "Daddy, it could be worse. Reynaud could be your son-in-law instead of Jay."

Horror crossed his face. "I changed my mind. You'll do, Gonzales."

Jay grunted. "Gee, thanks."

Shaw touched my cheek. "You called me Daddy. I dinnae think I'd ever hear that from yer lips again."

I hugged him once more. "I'm sorry about Mom, and what Reynaud said."

"I knew she was nae my mate. But I dinnae know she went back to him," he said, glancing away. "And I dinnae know the babe was nae mine. It wouldnae have mattered to me. I'd have loved him just the same as if he were my own."

"He's like a walking romance book hero," said Lindsay, staring at my father. "Does he have a brother?"

"Aye," he said with a laugh. "But I think yer husband would take exception to you being introduced to my brothers."

"Speaking of my husband," she said, before turning and opening the front door.

Exavier was there, with his cousin Eion. Exavier's hand was up as if he was just about to knock. "Lindsay, you cannot flash away from me when you don't like what I'm saying."

He came in; so did Eion.

I gave my father a good squeeze and then went to Jay. He slinked an arm around my waist, backing us up to get everyone inside.

Lindsay put a hand on her stomach again. "Oh, I didn't do that. Your child did. Apparently, the baby was sick of hearing you moan and groan too."

Eion snorted, and then put his hands up when Exavier rounded on him. "What? Come on. Your kid isn't even here yet and already it's that powerful. Imagine temper tantrums later. The kid will end up in another country."

Shaw grunted. "Aye. Gina did that to me once. She dinnae like being told no about making stakes when she was three. I told her it was dangerous. She got mad and then vanished into thin air. Scared a hundred years off me. Christian found her in my closet, her arms over her chest, her gaze hard. She was mad at me for days."

"You can vanish and travel that way?" asked Myra?

I shook my head. "No."

"Aye," said my father. "She was able to do so from birth. 'Tis nae something I can even do with ease. My mother could. And two of my brothers are able. Gina cannae shift forms to wolf though. The wolf is but a small portion of her. Her mother's temper and hair color took root deep. And her mother's slayer side. As noted by her being three and wanting to make stakes. Thankfully, she only had access to a plastic knife for modeling clay. I do nae want to think what she'd have done with access to anything else. She'd have whittled an arsenal."

Myra and Lindsay stared at me.

I shrugged. "I don't remember that, and I haven't vanished that I know of."

"Gina, your dad is a wolf shifter who can wield magik?" asked Myra.

I nodded.

Her lip curled. "Pity. The whole wolf thing does take away from the hot factor."

My father snorted.

I looked at him. "She's a cat shifter."

Jay hugged me to him and kissed the top of my head. "Baby, I love you, but should I hide the knives in the house? I'm not sure I want to walk in on you making stakes."

Lindsay burst into tears.

Exavier hugged her. "Honey, I know you're happy for them, but don't cry."

"You were right. They are so perfect together," she said, sinking into her husband's embrace.

Eion shook his head and walked around them both, extending his hand to my father. "Nice to meet you. I'm Eion, and the guy who looks confused by his pregnant wife's mood swings is Xavier."

"I'm fully planning to lecture my wife about showing up here without me," said Exavier. "I told her Eion and I were coming to help. She didn't think that was good enough."

I grinned.

Romeo came into the room with the ice cream and thrust it at Lindsay.

She took it and wasted no time eating it. With a mouthful, she spoke to Romeo. "I knew there was a reason I always liked you better than Jay."

Jay groaned.

Myra patted Exavier's shoulder. "Now that the women are all here, let's catch us up on what's happening and then let's kick some ass and take some names."

I smiled. "I think we need to call in Zachariah."

25

THE WAREHOUSE DISTRICT SEEMED EVEN MORE desolate and neglected than normal. I wasn't sure that was even possible. It was as if all the supernatural lawbreakers had heard something big was about to go down and they didn't want any part of it.

I couldn't blame them.

If I didn't have skin in the game, I'd have wanted far from it all too.

But backing down wasn't an option.

Reynaud had to be stopped. His reign of terror needed to come to an end.

We'd spent an entire day at Jay's house, trying to organize a plan of attack. Zachariah had arrived before the sun had come up, and he'd taken the steps needed to reach out to the local dens. All were on board to help in the fight against Reynaud. Apparently, they didn't appreciate the increase in crime either. It made going about their regularly scheduled programming harder to do with everyone watching.

Exavier had sent word through the local Fae community that there was a battle coming and they'd be needed. And the rest of Jay's pack had been notified. They all wanted to help. Fringe groups of supernaturals had reached out throughout the day, calling or coming to Jay's home, offering to assist.

None of them wanted Reynaud or his darkness in their city or possibly influencing them too.

Even the slayers that I'd never considered myself close to had arrived, wanting to help. They'd lost fellow sisters to the madman and two of their own were still missing. They wanted blood for it. I couldn't blame them.

I wasn't sure we'd ever actually agreed on any one plan. Finally, the idea of having me be bait came into play. Much to my father and my husband's dismay. It took some convincing, but I finally managed to persuade them to let me go to the club myself to draw out Reynaud. They'd only truly conceded when Myra insisted on accompanying me. I took my wins where I could and the moment the sun set we set out for the club.

Had we tried to go earlier, Zachariah and the vampires he was bringing to the battle wouldn't have been able to join us. Their numbers were great, and they could fight on Reynaud's level.

Vampire to vampire.

Myra touched my shoulder and glanced off to her right, looking into the blackness in the distance as we stood in the parking lot of Reynaud's club. It was dimly lit, adding to the ominous vibe it had going.

She sighed. "Remember how I mentioned I didn't think any of the men would listen and stay away long enough for us to draw out Reynaud?"

Groaning, I looked in the direction her attention was pulled to. "How many ignored us?"

"From the smell of it. All of them," said Myra, her gaze sliding to me. "I'm shocked they made it a whole two minutes before blatantly throwing our well-thought plan out the window. Men. They're infuriating."

Romeo stepped out from the darkness, his hands in the air as if signaling surrender.

I'd last seen him in Jay's kitchen where we'd all stood together formulating a plan to try to end Reynaud. Clearly, the men thought the plan was shit and formulated one of their own.

Since they were the types to let testosterone guide their actions, I wasn't holding out a lot of hope they'd do anything more than get in the way.

I eyed Romeo. "You draw the short straw?"

"I volunteered in hopes the ice cream bond we share would keep me safe from your wrath," he said.

I snorted.

"Think the creepy vamp guy will come now?" asked Myra, her hand still on my shoulder.

Suddenly, pain lanced through the bite marks Reynaud had given me. They each started to burn. Hissing, I tugged at the collar of my T-shirt. "Yep. I think he'll show. In fact, I'm sure of it."

Myra sniffed me. "You smell like a vampire suddenly."

I rubbed the spot Reynaud had bitten me the deepest. "Pretty sure he's flexing his power muscles as we speak."

Romeo neared us more, his hands still in the air.

Myra snorted. "Wolf-boy, you can put down the white flag. We won't kill you for being the guys' sacrificial lamb."

Romeo lowered his hands and then stopped, glancing around. "What is that?"

The same darkness I felt around Reynaud before began to creep over the area. It seemed to emanate from the club itself. I could feel it slinking its way over the ground, searching out something or someone. It zeroed in on Romeo and I inhaled sharply.

So did he.

"Kill me if I try to hurt you," he said as it slammed into him.

Myra let her claws emerge from her hands.

I gasped. "You can't really kill him."

"What is one less wolf-shifter?" she asked with a shrug.

I grabbed her arm but looked at Romeo. "Oracle, you still you?"

He patted himself, going so far as to feel his groin as well. "Yes. Pretty sure I'm still me."

"Want to tear my head off?" I asked.

"Nope. I want to take you back to Jay's and make you sit tight while we handle this."

I exhaled. "Yeah, sure sign you're not mind-jacked. The other idiots can come out now. I promise not to bite."

Jay rushed out from the darkness, followed closely by Shaw and the others.

Exavier twisted. "That is a shit load of evil I'm feeling. More than any one master vampire should be capable of."

Shaw nodded. "Aye. He made a deal with darkness long ago. I do nae know the price, but I know it's pure evil and powerful."

Exavier looked to Jay. "This isn't like anything I've encountered before. And it doesn't feel natural."

Romeo nodded. "Gina mentioned that she thought it felt like it didn't come *from* Reynaud but to him, kind of. As if its separate from him."

Exavier put his hands out and turned in a slow circle.

I could sense the power trickling over him, curious but tentative in regard to him. Interesting. It must have sensed who he was and what he was capable of.

"Exavier," I said. "I get the feeling it's not so sure it wants to take you on."

He shivered. "I feel like someone walked over my grave."

The bite marks on me hurt more. I hissed and grabbed my neck.

Jay and Shaw came right for me.

Grunting, Jay pushed past Shaw and pulled me to him. Jay turned me to face him. "Gina? What is it? I can feel your pain. Tell me what hurts."

"Where he bit me burns."

Shaw stiffened. "He's calling you to him, lass. Do nae give into the lure."

I met his gaze. "I think we're safe from me falling into his arms. He makes my skin crawl."

"Guid," returned Shaw, edging closer to me.

Myra snorted. "Gina, you do realize that between your mate and your father, you won't be standing against anything. I'm shocked they didn't lock you in the cell at Jay's place like they threatened to do to Lindsay if she attempted to follow."

Romeo groaned and rubbed his forehead.

"What?" I asked.

He motioned to Jay. "He's totally regretting not doing that. Dumbass."

There was a swooshing noise, and I turned slightly to find Zachariah there. He nodded to Exavier before turning his attention to Jay.

Jay growled slightly. "You should have told me about the attack on her the night you sent her to the club."

"I know," said Zachariah. "But be honest. You'd have launched a war."

Romeo nodded. "Oh yeah. Big time."

"For sure," said Samuel, approaching from the other side of the parking lot. Mason and Christian were close by his side.

With a long, annoyed breath, I looked at Jay. "Tell me you at least left someone at your house to guard Lindsay and the baby."

Exavier grinned. "Eion is there as well as the rest of my band. Nothing is getting past them."

I almost felt bad for anything that tried since his bandmates were all high-guards of the Dark Fae.

"I should probably confess a new development," said Zachariah.

I sighed. "Bigger than finding out my dad is the Scottish dude?"

Shaw waggled his brows.

Zachariah did a double-take and then cleared his throat. "Well, no, not that big, but it's something. I believe Reynaud may have succeeded in converting Tabitha and Lucy."

I tensed. "He turned two slayers into vampires? What? No way."

Zachariah faced me. "He has the power to do so. And more than one report of them being seen feeding on humans has come in tonight. I have slayers looking into it, but I ordered them to stay far from the club. I won't risk anymore being turned."

Jay held me tighter to him. "You're saying that he's probably got slayers on his side in addition to like a hundred vampires and pure evil?"

Zachariah rubbed his jaw. "Yes. That sums it up nicely."

"Not to mention he can apparently mind-jack people," added Myra, not really helping with easing the tension any.

"Lass, if his darkness is here, he cannae be

too far," said Shaw. "Take the females and go. Let us handle this matter."

Myra tipped her head, a hand going to her hip. "Listen here, hunk. You're hot but I'm not taking a backseat to this prick who dared to hurt my friend. And I know Gina. She won't back down either."

"This is nae up for debate," snapped Shaw. "Gonzales, tell them I'm right."

Jay opened his mouth, took one look at Myra and then me and snapped his mouth shut.

Shaw grunted. "Yer weak, Gonzales."

"Having a healthy fear of my mate isn't weak," said Jay before caressing my hip. "Baby, please go. We can handle this."

A black mist filled the entire area. When it cleared the parking lot was packed with vampires. None of them looked to be on our side.

I felt him then. Reynaud was close, watching me.

Jay growled so loudly that I was sure people in a four-block radius probably thought a massive animal got loose from a zoo. That or they were all supernatural and knew one badass alpha shifter was pissed.

Two women I knew well stepped out from the seemingly endless group of vampires.

Zachariah drew in a deep breath.

So did I.

He was right. Tabitha and Lucy were converted as noted by the fangs they flashed at us. While I'd never particularly liked them, I'd never wished this fate upon them. And if I wouldn't have seen it with my own eyes, I'd have never believed converting a slayer into a vampire was even possible.

Lucy stepped forward, her short dark hair spiked up in all directions. Her smile was wide, but the look in her eyes was wild. "Things were good until you got here, Gina. We were Zacharias' favorites." She motioned to Tabitha, who held a knife in her hand.

Both women wore stakes and knives attached to each thigh.

Tabitha nodded. "You came along and everything changed. It's been nothing but Regina this and Regina that."

Zachariah stepped forward more. "That is not true. I value you both. Reynaud plants the seeds of jealousy in you, knowing you are too new to the demon in you to resist. You can fight his hold on you even though he sired you both. Focus and break his will."

They didn't look like they wanted to break anything other than our faces.

"Zachariah," said another slayer I knew well from behind us.

I glanced over my shoulder to find every slayer from our division there, closing ranks along with what I could only guess were the vampires Zachariah had called in to help.

Jay's pack appeared as well, each looking ready to fight to the death for the cause.

One by one Fae males began to pop up at seemingly random spots. The more I thought about it all, the less random and more strategic their positioning appeared to be.

It took me a moment to recognize that while I'd assumed I was alone in the world, I wasn't. Each and every one of these people came to help something that was a direct threat to me.

Myra touched my shoulder lightly. "Any sign of Creepy McCreepy?"

"Not yet," I returned, the bite area hurting once more. "But I know he's close."

In the next second, Reynaud appeared on the top of the club.

"Speak of the devil," I managed.

Myra snorted. "You weren't kidding. He *is* full of himself. Though, I'd have thought he'd be uglier. Shame to waste a perfectly good hot male to darkness, but whatever. Win some. Lose some. But hey, your dad is hot enough to make up for it all."

I nearly gagged.

She laughed.

Reynaud soaked in the sight of the army ready to stand against him. The crazy bastard smiled as if he'd been expecting something like this all along.

If he had, we'd played right into his hands. And by *we* I meant the dumbass men who decided to toss the playbook out the window.

"Ladies," he said to Tabitha and Lucy, who looked totally enamored by his very presence.

Yuck.

They sneered before glancing at all of the vampires surrounding us. "Kill them all and take Gina to the master. I'm told she'll make a grand companion and mother to his children."

"He'll nae touch my daughter!" yelled Shaw.

"I'll rip your fucking head off, Reynaud!"

Jay jerked me behind him and put his hands out to each side of me and let them shift. Fur covered his forearms and hands while huge claws emerged from his fingertips. The snarl that tore free from him left no room for interpretation.

Fuck with his wife and die.

My husband was fierce.

So was I.

Every one of the good guys took a fighting stance and the enemy didn't disappoint. They launched a full-scale attack. The ground seemed to shake as supernatural collided against supernatural. It was epic and chaotic.

I went low while Jay went high. We cut through the enemy with ease at first, neither taking any hits. It took me a moment to realize that Jay and I worked together as if we'd been doing it for years and years, when in truth, we rarely did.

The happy thought left quickly when I realized just how many vampires were coming at us. They seemed to be multiplying.

The darkness that covered the ground increased and rushed up my legs, halting my movements. A vampire slammed into me and

Myra attacked it, beheading it before grabbing for me. She tugged, I remained planted in place.

Her eyes widened. "Gina?"

Jay twisted, and his brows met. "Baby?"

"I can't move," I said, my voice barely there.

He paled and rushed me, trying to lift me but he couldn't. I was stuck to the ground as if I was a cement statue.

Shaw appeared and cut through two more of the enemy. "Lass?"

"I can't fucking move her!" yelled Jay, sounding panicked.

The same static energy I'd felt while Jay was claiming me rushed through once again. One second, I was there, near my husband, in the center of the battle and the next, Jay and I were in a darkened hall that looked to be carved deep in the earth.

Jay spun. "What the hell?"

I lifted a foot, happy to see I could move again. "Jayson? Where are we?"

He grabbed my hand. "No fucking clue."

The darkness level increased in the area so much so that I honestly wondered if we were standing in hell.

Jay sniffed and then gasped. "Gina, I think we're under the club. In the den."

I eased closer to him. "How did we get here?"

He closed his eyes a second. "Baby, remember how your father told me you flashed away from him when he wouldn't let you make stakes when you were little?"

I thought about it and then sucked in a huge breath. "Holy shit balls, I brought us here?"

He nodded. "That is my guess."

The urge to move down the corridor was great. I gave in and dragged Jay with me. As we came to a fork in the tunnels, I paused.

Something snarled and leaped out at me.

Jay killed it before I could blink.

He looked down at the dead vampire and then put his hands on my shoulders. "You lead, I'll follow."

I did.

He stuck to me like glue.

The corridor opened into a large room and in the center of it was a pedestal. On it was what looked like a snow globe. If snow globes held blue fire and felt like death the closer you got to them.

My eyes widened. "I think that is the darkness. At least the source of it."

Jay went for it and I grabbed his arm.

"I'm not sure we should touch it," I said.

He bent, touched my chin, kissed my lips and winked. In the next breath, the fool not only grabbed the glass ball, he threw it at the wall. It shattered and blue light went everywhere.

Jay threw me to the floor and covered me with his body.

I screamed, sure he was going to burn away to nothing more than ash. When I realized he was not only in one piece but apparently unharmed, I slapped the crap out of his arms. The bite marks Reynaud had given me stopped hurting instantly.

Jay grunted and rolled off me before helping me to my feet.

I slapped him again for good measure once I was standing.

He grinned. "What?"

"Jayson, what if that would have killed you?"

"Your father would kill Reynaud and you'd be safe. Without me, but safe," he said calmly.

I hit him again.

He flinched. "Ouch."

I stilled. "You didn't like end the outside world or anything, did you?"

He paused, concern flashing through his brown gaze.

I groaned. "You went all alpha and acted without thinking. Jayson, if you ended the world I'm going to be so pissed."

He bit his lower lip. "Um, okay."

The was a popping noise and Exavier was suddenly there. He stared around the cavern. "Are you two okay?"

I gave Jay a hard look. "Yes, by the grace of the gods because dumbass here just took what I'm fairly sure was a globe of pure darkness and threw it at the wall. Tell me there is a world left out there."

Exavier stared at Jay. "That huge flux of evil was because of you?"

Jay blushed. "Erm, yes."

Exavier rolled his eyes.

I stared at him.

"The world is still out there. A mass of darkness rushed over the area and then vanished. The second it did, Reynaud looked scared shitless." He looked at me. "Gina, your dad moved faster than I've ever seen anyone move. One second he was close to Myra and the next he was next to Reynaud."

"Is he okay?" I asked, scared for my father.

"If by okay you mean standing on a pile of ashes that used to be Reynaud, while singing some song in what I'm guessing is Gaelic, then yes. He's totally fine," said Exavier.

I gasped. "Reynaud is dead?"

Exavier nodded.

Jay spun around, lifted me and hugged me tight enough to crush me.

I winced.

He let up and set me on my feet. "I'm starting to like your father more and more."

Exavier grunted. "Not sure you're growing on him any. Plus, you're going to have to tell him you knocked up his daughter."

I swayed. "What?"

Exavier glanced at me and then focused on my stomach. "I just spoiled the surprise, didn't I?"

I turned and swatted Jay some more.

He laughed and lifted me again, kissing me thoroughly. "Mmm, Fiery One, how about we go out, and I'll help finish off the bad guys while you stand out of the way and look sexy and pregnant."

I glared at him.

"You're super-hot when you're pissed at me."

Exavier laughed. "Come on. Let's go finish off the last of Reynaud's vampires and go back to your place so I can try to calm my wife down. Just think now we'll have two lethal hormonal women to contend with."

Jay set me down gently and cupped himself. "Shit."

"Yeah, shit," said Exavier laughing.

I took Jay's hand in mine. "Bet you're sorry you claimed me, aren't you?"

He grinned. "Hell no! I love you, woman, even though you're the most stubborn woman I've ever met."

"I love you too even though you could have ended the world a few minutes ago."

"Uh, let's not tell your father about that. I'm already batting a thousand with him," said Jay, making Exavier and I laugh.

I stilled. "What happens now?"

Jay winked. "Now the boys and me kick some ass and then I figure out how to best hide from a wolf-shifter who wields magik. Fun times."

THE END

WANT to read Exavier and Lindsay's story? Check out Loup Garou by Mandy M. Roth

ABOUT THE AUTHOR

Dear Reader

Did you enjoy this title and want to know more about Mandy M. Roth, her pen names and all the titles she has available for purchase (over 100)?

About Mandy:

New York Times & *USA TODAY* Bestselling Author Mandy M. Roth is a self-proclaimed Goonie, loves 80s music and movies and wishes leg warmers would come back into fashion. She also thinks the movie The Breakfast Club should be mandatory viewing for...okay, everyone. When she's not dancing around her office to the sounds of the 80s or writing books, she can be found designing book covers for New York publishers, small presses, and indie authors.

Learn More:

To learn more about Mandy and her pen names, please visit http://www.mandyroth.com

For latest news about Mandy's newest releases and sales subscribe to her newsletter

To join Mandy's Facebook Reader Group: The Roth Heads, please visit

https://www.facebook.com/groups/MandyRothReaders/

Review this title:

Please let others know if you enjoyed this title. Consider leaving an honest review on the vendor site in which you purchased this title. Reviews help to spread the word and boost overall sales. This means more books in the series you love.

Thank you!

CPSIA information can be obtained
at www.ICGtesting.com
Printed in the USA
LVHW090407210520
656071LV00009B/695

9 781986 240987